Artists' Tales

By Joseph Meigs

PRESS

The Black Mountain Press
109 Roberts Street,
Asheville, NC 28801

Artist Tales

copyright © 2015 by Joseph Meigs
Printed in the USA

Short Stories
by **Joseph Meigs**

ISBN: 9781940605944

The Black Mountain Press
109 Roberts Street, Asheville, NC 28801

First Printing, November 2015
10 9 8 7 6 5 4 3 2 1
Library of Congress Control Number: 2015910937

Printed in the United States of America
Cover Design: Cynthia Potter
Cover Photo: Joseph Meigs

PUBLISHER'S NOTE
This is a work of fiction. Names, characters, places, and incidents are either the product of the author's imagination or are used fictitiously.

*For friends and
family who encouraged me
in my creative endeavors.*

Table of Contents

01
The Calling

I was always fascinated by people who thought they had received a vocational calling. They usually ended up being clergymen, teachers, doctors, nurses, or some other altruistic server of the greater community, claiming that some force of nature or even God almighty had done the calling, though I suspected that, if a deity were involved, it was the god of money or status who rang them up. Incidentally, I never met a lawyer who claimed to be called to his profession, at least not by God.

I longed to have the call—from any source—believing that finding my assigned slot in life would give me a sense of purpose and power. I temporarily held a couple of jobs that I thought I was chosen for, first working for a humane society and then serving as a substitute teacher, but neither job lasted more than a few months. And I have taken a couple of other jobs I've known to have nothing to do with a vocational calling. The first was dealing cards in a casino, where the only "call" was the one made in poker. The other is my current one as a loan officer at a small local bank in Waynesville, North Carolina. With both jobs I've worried that God—if He or She did issue my call—might be angry with me for shirking my real task in life and, after placing me on a boat, cause a storm, whereupon the other passengers would toss me overboard and I would end up in a whale.

However, a day came in the spring of last year that put me, I believe, on the path to my true calling. It was the day I purchased a set of previously owned watercolors from a small emporium called The Last One Standing. This peculiar establishment was located on a back street—more of an alley than a street—off Biltmore Avenue in Asheville, about twenty miles from my house in Waynesville. I was attracted to the shop because there were several portrait paintings hanging in the front window, one of which reminded me of the figure in Munch's *The Scream*.

Inside, on high shelves, sat life-like dolls, most of which were punctured with long needles and pins. On lower shelves rested an array of vials, bottles, and jars, filled with variously colored liquids that I took to be potions and elixirs. From the ceiling hung an assortment of amulets, charms, and talismans. On a strangely carved pedestal, shaped like a raven's head, sat an incense burner, which filled the room with an acrid smoke that smelled a bit like smoldering tarpaper. On the counter rested a shriveled apple with two bites out of it.

After several minutes of seeing no one, I was on the verge of leaving, when seemingly from nowhere a man of indeterminable age appeared beside me. His face was dotted with bad acne that looked like corn kernels stuck on his skin. His left sideburn was longer and thicker than his right one, making his head seem to be permanently cocked to one side. "Looking for anything in particular?" he asked, as he began cleaning his long fingernails with a pop top from an aluminum can.

"Not really. I just saw paintings in the front window and thought I'd look around. I've nearly exhausted my supply of watercolor paints and hoped I could find some replacements."

"Here, take a look at these," he said, leading me to the front counter, where, next to the apple, sat a box of paints, ones I had not noticed moments before. Judging by the partially squeezed in sides, the tubes of paints were second-hand, but whoever had owned them had used only a minimal amount of each one, and they included most of the colors I like to use, including raw umber, burnt sienna, ochre, sepia, and lamp black.

So, even though they weren't my usual Grumbacher paints, being instead a brand I did not recognize—Thanadiem—I felt like they were a

by Joseph Meigs

bargain at $10. "I'll take them," I declared.

After ringing up the sale, the clerk laughed and said, "Thank you, Mr. Stauf. I think you'll get lots of use out of these."

"I'm sure I will," I responded, "but how did you know my name?"

"You must have told me when you came in. John Stauf, isn't it?"

"Yes, but I don't remember . . . ."

"Well," he interrupted, "is there anything else I can help you with?"

"No, these will do." As I turned to leave, I asked, "What's with the apple?"

"Oh, just a souvenir from the past," he said.

Within a week of the purchase—ironically in the early spring–I completed a painting of a maple tree on Highway 19 outside Waynesville. The tree grew on the edge of a fertile looking field that, when summertime came, was usually dominated by thistle, ironweed, and Queen Anne's lace. I was attracted to the proliferation of small red maple buds that served as precursors to green maple leaves of summer and eventually red leaves of fall. However, though the tree had appeared to be healthy enough when I did the painting, it never advanced beyond the bud stage and began dying, a process I witnessed as I drove by the field daily on my way to work. Once it was clear that the tree would not revive, the owner quickly cut it down, I guess to prevent its falling over and blocking the adjacent gravel road. I hung the painting in my bedroom.

I next put the paints to use on a scene of a waterfront house at Wrightsville Beach, North Carolina, where I stayed for a week in early July, enjoying summer weather conducive to playing golf on several of the nearby coastal courses and to relaxing in the sand. In one of my industrious surges, I completed a twelve by eighteen watercolor of the house, spending a whole day on the details of the weathered wood, the front porch swing, the red shutters, and the sea oats running down the side. I hung the painting in my study over my computer desk.

Less than a week later, after reading in the paper that Wrightsville Beach had been struck by Hurricane Bertha, I called the owner to make sure that the house was all right and to see if I could rent it again in the late fall. With sadness in his voice, he informed me that the house had faced the full force of the hurricane and that, once the roof and front wall had blown off, the rest of the place followed suit in a matter of minutes.

My subsequent painting was a barn, one located not far from the maple that died. I chose the barn for its combination of strength and fragility. Oak lumber gave it an aura of sturdiness, while missing boards and a definite sagging to the right gave it an air of vulnerability. Through the gaps I could see old tools and farm equipment—a hay rake, shovels, pitchforks, and the like. On pegs outside hung a couple of harnesses in need of saddle soap. A large plow lay in the grass at the base of the front wall. The painting took me about three evenings to complete. I hung it in my living room over the fireplace.

A few days later, I happened to be driving down Highway 19 after a particularly violent thunderstorm, only to discover the barn on fire, seemingly hit by lightning, even though it sat low, surrounded by a number of tall trees. Two or three drivers had pulled their cars off the road to watch the conflagration, one of which had already called 911. The barn burned to the ground before the fire department arrived, taking with it the farm equipment.

Still not totally believing in magical powers, I painted my first animal with the Thanadiem paints while sitting at the dining room table of my own house, using a photograph I had taken earlier of a hawk. I had often seen the bird soaring high above my property and had even heard his shrill whistle—probably to its mate or, maybe, to its potential prey, saying in effect, "I'm bad. I can let you know that I'm here and I'm still going to nail you." I fondly named the hawk Billy Jack, after the movie character, who told his adversary, as best I can remember, "I'm going to take my foot and hit you up side of your head, and there's nothing you can do about it."

One day, when I was turning into my driveway, I spotted Billy Jack on a tree limb within ten yards or so of me. Twice he spread his wings and half hopped, half flew to a different branch, revealing an irregular set of tail feathers. I happened to have my camera in the car and, using my telephoto lens, snapped a good picture of him the second time he changed branches with his wings spread. Later, I used the photograph as the basis of a sixteen by twenty painting, which now hangs in my dining room, overlooking a bowl of wooden fruit.

Three or four days after finishing the painting, I was sitting in my living room, reading Stephen King's *Misery*. I live in an L-shaped house that has a lot of glass facing out onto a patio. In the past I often had to nurse back to health birds that had flown into the glass or bury those that did not survive the crash. Suddenly, I heard, if my onomatopoetic ear serves me correctly, first a thud, then a loud whump. On the porch lay a sparrow—stunned, but seemingly alive. Next to it sprawled an obviously dead hawk, in fact, Billy Jack, judging by the irregular tail feathers. He was now grotesquely changed from when I had photographed and painted him. Eventually, the sparrow flew away, maybe to become an avian evangelist, testifying about its near death experience to groups of other birds, and even some deer and chipmunks, gathered at woodland tent revivals. The next day, after waiting futilely for Billy Jack to come back to life, I buried him in the small pet cemetery I now managed in the back yard.

When Winston Plutarch offered me $400 to do a portrait of his wife Mildred, I hesitated, wondering if I should inform him of my artistic bad luck, or rather the bad luck of the subjects of my paintings. I decided not to mention it, not so much because I thought that he would actually believe I might curse his wife by painting her, but because I was afraid that he would think I was a crazy person, deluded into believing I had mystical powers. In either case, I was sure he would withdraw his offer and I'd be out $400. Besides, I was beginning to like the feeling I got when I painted with the Thanadiem paints, convinced that I was painting better than ever before.

To ease my conscience, I did inform him that I had never done a human portrait, but he had seen my other paintings and was confident I could do justice to his wife.

Mildred sat for me three evenings in her living room, with Winston hovering nearby, watching my every stroke, commenting often on my technique. I finally took a series of photographs of her so that I could work in private. If I say so myself, the finished product was commendable, capturing on watercolor paper her auburn hair, dark brown eyes, and high cheekbones, plus I worked in, for background purposes, a few flowers, a couple with bees on them, as if she were sitting outside on a spring day. She was a fine looking woman to begin with, but my painting flattered her, particularly around her mouth and eyes, as I omitted lots of small lines. Winston seemed pleased, as did Mildred. They hung the painting in their living room. I spent the $400 on a set of new irons endorsed by Jack Nicklaus, an indulgence I had previously considered forbidden because of the price.

A whole month went by, and I neither heard nor read about any Mildred mishaps. I figured that I had overestimated my control—or rather the paint's control—over the fate of my subjects. I was back to believing that all had been coincidental and that the power of the paints had been specious.

I was thus taken by surprise when, a few days after the month's end, I got a note from Winston informing me that Mildred had died a horrible death, due to a severe allergic reaction to a bee sting. She and Winston had hiked into a meadow for a picnic, and she had forgotten to take an antihistamine with her, even though she had a history of extreme reactions when stung. He tried to haul her to the car, but stumbled on a root and twisted his ankle. He said he felt guilty, but then he told me that he was grateful I had captured her beauty before she died. I wondered if the value of my painting had gone up.

For several months after the Mildred episode, I avoided painting anything live, including Winston's cousin, who admired the painting of Mildred so much she wanted me to do one of her, with Winston's blessing. Instead, I did only still life paintings, including cut flowers, which would die anyway, and inanimate objects, including a bowl, a vase, and on a larger scale, a freestanding chimney that was the only remnant of a house that had burned down some time in the past. I even did these paintings as abstracts, hoping I could trick the Watercolor Grim Reaper, but all I did was delay the inevitable. The flowers did die, of course, but in a way so did the bowl and the vase, both of which developed cracks about a month after I did the paintings, such that they would never again hold water. The chimney collapsed into a heap of rubble.

It all confirmed my suspicion that there was a relationship between the details in the painting and the elapsed time before the subject succumbed—the more accurate the representation, the quicker the demise. Flattering Mildred in the painting might have delayed her inevitable death, just as the abstract painting delayed the cracks in the bowl and vase and the collapse of the chimney.

My conscience began to bother me, and I thought about throwing the paints away. But then I decided to return them to The Last One Standing, where I hoped to at least get my ten dollars back. I drove over on a Saturday morning, carrying the paints in a freezer baggie. The same strange, acne-marred man again appeared. "I'm having a problem with these paints you sold me," I said.

"Are they not the colors you expected? Do they not mix well with water?" he asked, picking up the shriveled apple I had seen before.

"No, they're great, the best I've used. In fact, they make me feel more . . . artistic, but . . . ."

"So, what's the problem then?" he asked.

I felt confused—and foolish. I did not want to admit that I believed that they had deadly power. After hesitating for a moment, while I tried to think of words that might sound plausible, I turned and walked out, taking the paints with me. I could not help but notice, as I looked back, that my indecisiveness and abrupt departure left the clerk with a wry smile.

Still feeling apprehensive about the paints, I did stop on the way home at a national chain art supply store and bought some Grumbacher watercolors, which I used for awhile, with nothing dramatic happening. This narrowed the possibilities of blame; it was either the Thanadiem paints or a combination of them and me that had the destructive power. At least for almost a month, I rested easy, knowing that, by not using the paints from The Last One Standing, I was not bringing further mayhem into the world.

But the urge to exert my power kept nagging me, and the day finally came when I returned to doing paintings with the Thanadiem paints. It was also the day that I consciously chose–with no guesswork–to do a painting that might bring about the death of the subject. It involved a dog appropriately named after the god of the underworld, Pluto, a mixed breed hell-hound with maybe some rottweiler in it, some Doberman, a trace of pit bull, owned by my next-door neighbor named Brad. Pluto barked incessantly, loudest between 12 midnight and 7 am, my prime sleeping hours. I tried running a fan to block out the harsh noise with "soft" noise, each night clicking the control to a higher speed, until the fan sounded like the engine of a prop-jet airplane. I could still hear the dog barking. So could my own small dog, Trax, who insisted on jumping on my bed whenever Pluto barked, thus succeeding in waking me up in the few moments when Pluto's barking failed to.

Finally, after four nights of virtual sleeplessness, I went to Brad's house to complain. It was after midnight, but the lights were on in every room, so I figured Brad was up. Pluto was lying at the base of the front stairs, barking without seeming to inhale. He stopped only to bare his teeth at me and rattle out a growl. He wore a large blue collar.

After edging around Pluto, whom I fully expected to lunge at me, I knocked at the door–several times in fact–before Brad appeared, dressed only in boxer shorts, holding a can of Old Milwaukee, scratching his butt. "Yeah, man, what's up?" he asked.

"It's about your dog."

"My dog? Pluto? You want him?"

"No, I've come to complain about his barking. I can't sleep at night because of all the noise."

"Have you tried shutting your windows?"

"It's summertime, and I don't have an air conditioner."

"Then you should try a fan. It works to block out noise."

"I did try that. It doesn't help, even on ultra-high speed."

"Then you ought to drink a few beers, before you go to bed, like me.

See." He held up the Old Milwaukee over his head. "I sleep like a baby—never even hear the dog."

"I'm sure."

Just then the phone rang. "Oops, gotta go." With that, Brad abruptly turned and entered his house. I waited two or three minutes and then gave up. As I walked from the stairs to the street, I heard Pluto growling, then felt a forceful tugging on the right pant leg of my jeans. Pluto had grabbed on and was shaking his head violently as if he were trying to snap the neck of a rodent he had caught. I got free by picking up a broom that was lying in the yard and swishing it at Pluto's head. As I hustled back to my house, the dog stood in the street barking at me.

As soon as I was safely in my living room, I began a painting of Pluto, from memory, trying to capture his appearance as he stood in the street—detailing his brown and black coat, his oversized head, his teeth, and blue collar. I must not have been terribly accurate in the depiction because I continued to hear him barking at all hours of the night for another two weeks or so, while the painting hung in my bathroom over the toilet.

But then one night the barking ceased. The next morning I went for a jog, starting out in Brad's—and Pluto's—direction. I quickly discovered Pluto lying dead on the side of the road, his head bent back as if he had been caught in mid-bark when he was hit. I figured he had been standing approximately in the same spot as the night I left him barking at me. For a moment, I felt sorry for Pluto. After studying him, I strode up to the house and banged on the door. When a sleepy-faced Brad appeared, I said, "Somebody must have run over your dog last night."

I was on the verge of denying that I was in any way responsible, when he spoke up. "I know," he said. "I'm the one that did it."

"YOU killed him!" I exclaimed. Somehow in my mind I had pictured a fast moving semi serving as Pluto's executioner.

"Yeah, I was coming home from a party last night—a bit too much to drink—didn't see the stupid bitch—must have been sitting right in the road—too tired to dig a grave right after it happened—do it this morning."

Surprised that Brad might not even know his own dog's gender, I left to take my intended jog, still thinking about my painting of Pluto. The longer I ran, the more I felt qualms about initiating Pluto's doom. I vowed not to use the paints again, at least for live subjects. On the other hand, I did wish that I had included Brad in the picture.

It was during my post-Pluto period that I pondered my role in all this. Why did I wind up with the deadly paints? Why were they for sale at The Last One Standing? Who had used them before me, and to what end? Why did the tubes of Thanadiem never seem to get used up? Was I being called to serve as a scourge of God to wipe out undesirables, like Pluto, and maybe also criminals, genocidal despots, and the like?

Some people might think I was overstepping my boundaries, but I decided to find the answer to this latter question. Using more of the Thanadiem watercolors, I painted portraits of people I believed to be evil. I first considered Pluto's master, Brad, but I couldn't really call him evil, even if he was an obnoxious boor. Besides, I had already punished him by painting Pluto, so I focused upon a couple of people I came to know through my job as loan officer at the bank. With them, I did not strive for accuracy, thus causing a fair measure of time to elapse between doing the painting and the eventually death. First came an obese, corrupt mayor, who was depositing way more money into his account than his salary would justify, a fact that I came to know—illegally, I admit—by looking at his bank statement. Using extra-strength wire for the large painting I did of him (a thirty by forty), I hung his likeness in my opening hallway, a spot befitting a person of his stature. He choked to death on a chicken bone at a picnic held by the local library to raise money for books.

The next painting was of a distinguished looking gentleman, Vincent Liotta, who, according to rumor, was a former crime boss that had escaped his seedy past through testifying against his old cronies and ending up in a witness relocation program. He often came into the bank and took out huge loans, promptly paying them back within a month or so. I never knew for sure if the rumors were true, but I did know that even though I did all the paperwork for him, he was never friendly to me, treating me as if I were merely a clerk. His painting hangs in my laundry room overlooking a shelf on which I keep a box of Tide. He died of a self-inflicted gunshot wound that occurred while he was cleaning a .38.

And there were others: a surly curmudgeon who screamed at kids in his neighborhood, whose painting hangs in my kitchen next to the microwave, who died of an aneurysm that hit him during one of his tirades after a soccer ball rolled into his yard; a teenager who often drove down my street with mega-speakers blasting out rap music, whose portrait graces the right wall of my garage, who died in a bungee jumping accident; and a former girl friend, Polly Klondike, who left me for her female roommate in college. Her painting hangs on the left side of the garage, facing the one of the rap-loving teenager. She died soon after the painting was completed of an undetermined disease, which I hope I didn't get.

Things started to come apart for me while I was gone on a four-day vacation, leaving my dog Trax in the care of an acquaintance named Jake. Jake apparently roamed through my house, making sure that Trax had not messed anywhere, but also taking note of the subjects of my latest paintings. He recognized several, from the news, as being recently deceased and observed the dates next to my signatures on the watercolors, indicating that the paintings had been done shortly before the deaths of the subjects. Jake must have mentioned the odd coincidences to his wife, who told her hairdresser, who was married to a Sheriff's Department detective named Armstrong, who showed up at the bank where I work, after I returned from my vacation. He looked, with his beard and curly hair, like the figure on the right side (looking out) of a box of Smith Brothers Cough Drops, except that his clothes looked tighter and his forehead more wrinkled than Mr. Smith's.

He asked me if he could see the paintings Jake had discovered. I agreed, not even asking if he had a search warrant, feeling confident that I had nothing to worry about, since all of the deaths had been ruled accidental or due to natural causes. After looking at the pictures of the mayor, the former crime boss, the grump, the teenager, and the former girlfriend, he asked, "Are there other paintings you want to show me, Mr. Stauf?"

"Nope, that's it," I responded. I didn't mention Mildred's portrait or comment on the fate of the tree, the hawk, the barn, the beach house, or Pluto.

"How comes it that you happened to paint these people, who, coincidentally, all ended up dead?" he asked.

"No big deal," I answered. "I've long admired the mayor, and I liked the gentlemanly profile of Mr. Liotta, but then I needed a couple of youthful figures to counterbalance the older men." I didn't tell him that I had dated the girl in the painting.

"According to the dates on the paintings, these people all died right after you painted them. Doesn't that strike you as particularly odd?"

"Yes, it certainly does. But, as I'm sure you are aware, there is no evidence connecting me to their actual deaths, unless you believe I have some magical powers to cause harm. Do you believe I have such powers, Detective Armstrong?"

"No, of course not," he asserted, forcefully enough to indicate a bit of doubt, though I could tell that he was a person who usually tried to come up with a rational explanation for everything.

After he left, I felt as if I were off the hook. I mean, what was he going to report to his fellow officers down at the Sheriff's Department, that I was practicing some kind of voodoo? They'd probably laugh at him. But then he showed up at the bank again two days later. "You didn't tell me that the woman, whose picture hangs in your garage, was once your girl friend."

"What difference would it have made?"

"It just makes everything seem to be a bit more than just coincidental, don't you agree?"

"Not really. Like I said, I just needed a pretty face on that side of the garage." I didn't tell him about her trading me in for her roommate.

After asking me several questions about my attitude toward my job, the people that had died, and my history as a painter, he left. As soon as Armstrong was out the door, the bank manager, Harold Phillips, called me into his office. He surface juggled three ball bearings in the palm of his right hand, tempting me to address him as Captain Queeg or Mr. Bogart. "I don't know what's going on," he said, "but it doesn't look good for the bank to have a policeman coming in here asking questions of one of our employees. Customers might get the wrong impression."

"What impression?" I asked.

"I don't know, but it can't be favorable. And besides, there are the other bank employees to consider. They're also uncomfortable with the police hanging around."

"I see." I looked out from Phillips' office through the glass partition and saw Janice Dwindler and Robert Popson, both standing at their teller stations, staring at me, as was Geraldine Perkins, the keeper of the safety deposit box keys, a woman whom I had asked out—and been rejected by— on several occasions. I didn't see June Bottoms or Dolly Dunkirk, but I was sure they would have been staring at me too if they were present. The only person who might have lent me any sympathy, Laura Wood, was not there that day, having stayed home to tend to her sick baby.

To make a long story short, I got fired, and that's when I decided to do a group painting.

I used as the basis for my project a photograph that had been taken of the staff in front of the bank on the day it was reopened after a remodeling job, shortly before I was hired. Figuring nobody would notice its absence, I stole the picture from off the top of the filing cabinet where it usually rested on a small easel, partially hidden by a fichus plant. After I finished the painting, I hung it in the attic. I then returned the photograph to its former spot behind the fichus.

Within a week, all the people in the painting except Geraldine died from an assortment of accidents and sudden illnesses, ranging from a ruptured appendix to heat stroke. Phillips led the *danse macabre* after stepping on a ball bearing and tumbling down his lengthy staircase. I must have painted him the most accurately.

But I made a serious mistake. When I set out to paint the different bank members, I assumed the rather large woman in the picture, wearing sunglasses, was Geraldine Perkins. I kept seeing Geraldine at the funeral services. She was remorseful but appeared perfectly healthy, first making me admire her constitution, then wonder how I slipped up in painting her.

After a week or so, I read that Laura Wood, the one member of the bank staff I purposefully tried to exclude from the group painting, had fallen off a balcony at a high-rise hotel. Geraldine attended her funeral also. Laura's death is what prompted me to go back and study carefully the photograph of the bank staff that I used for the painting. It was at that moment that I discovered the terrible error. The large woman in the photograph wearing sunglasses was not Geraldine Perkins at all, but in fact was Laura Wood, a fact that I should have ascertained by noting the small lapel button bearing a peace sign, which Laura wore almost every day to work. I was fooled by the fact that Laura had been seven months pregnant when the picture was taken, making her appear to be as large as Geraldine. The sunglasses had also tricked me. Geraldine apparently was not even at work the day the photograph was taken.

I was distraught—for two reasons. First, I had caused the death of someone I actually liked. The rest of the group didn't matter, but Laura had never harmed me. And, second, I was now aware that I—or the paints—could be destructive in ways that I did not intend. It made me think that if I could cause the death of someone like Laura, I could inadvertently cause the death of someone I considered to be far more important: me.

I vowed to take the paints back to The Last One Standing, which I did two days later, right after I painted a portrait of Geraldine Perkins, for whom I needed no photograph to work from, having seen her so many times at the funerals of her co-workers. I hung her painting in the attic next to the group picture.

The acne-covered young man still worked at the shop. He smiled knowingly as I entered, as if he had anticipated my reappearance. "How might I help you, Mr. Stauf?" he asked, placing his left hand on the twice-bitten, shriveled apple.

"I'd like to return these paints. I . . .I don't have any use for them anymore."

"You're sure about that?"

"Yes, I'm sure. I don't want to see them again."

"Lost control of them, have you?"

"No . . . .yes . . . I don't want to talk about it; I just want to return them."

"All right, since the tubes seem to be in the same condition as when you bought them, I'll pay you exactly what you originally paid for them. I believe it was ten dollars."

"No, you don't need to pay me for them. I just want you to take them back."

"We insist on paying for them. We're not a charity organization, you know. But I suspect you will want them again some time in the future. Be warned, however; they'll cost you a lot more than the ten dollars. We like to call this set 'The Chaser.' And also be warned that if you come back for them, they'll be with you for the rest of your life." He then handed me a ten-dollar bill, which I put in my pocket.

"Don't worry," I said. "I won't be needing them again."

"That remains to be seen," he replied. "Now, if you'll excuse me, I have other fish to fry." As he turned away, he said, "See you soon."

On the way home, I picked up a local newspaper, which contained an article about the tragic coincidence of the bank's employees all dying within a week or so of each other, the latest one being Geraldine Perkins, who died in a car wreck as she drove to visit the gravesite of Harold Phillips, the deceased bank manager, with whom, according to the report, she was having an affair. No wonder she kept turning me down.

Accompanying the article was a picture of Detective Armstrong, who had been assigned to investigate the unusual case. I tore out the picture and put it in my wallet, for what reason, I was not exactly sure, though it seemed like a good idea at the time. As I halfway expected, Detective Armstrong was waiting at my house when I arrived back from my visit to The Last One Standing.

"What can I do for you, Detective Armstrong?" I asked.

"I'd like to see your latest paintings."

"Interested in art, are you Detective?"

"No . . . murder. Could I look around your house again? If need be, I can get a warrant, you know."

"That won't be necessary," I answered, while I wondered where he would find a judge who would sign a search warrant based upon the notion that I had painted people to death. I showed him around the house, where he saw for the second time the paintings pre-dating the bank group portrait.

"What's up there?" he asked pointing to the pull-down door leading to the attic.

"Only an attic," I answered.

"Let's have a look," he stated, and we did, immediately finding my most recent art.

"How do you explain the fact that you did paintings of your fellow bank employees and they all recently died, just like all those others before?" he asked.

"I can't; I'm only a painter. They were simply my co-workers."

"Why is there a separate one of Geraldine Perkins?"

"Because I kind of liked her."

"You know of course that she died last evening?"

"I know! I read about it in the newspaper. I felt terrible about it."

I could tell that Armstrong did not believe me, judging by his snorts of derision, but then his snorts turned to dead silence when I said, "By the way, that was a nice picture of you in the paper." He left quickly, after telling me not to leave town and to come down to the station the next morning.

Before going to the station, however, I did leave town—a trip to Asheville.

Again, the acne-faced man at The Last One Standing greeted me as if he were expecting me. The Thanadiem paints sat on the counter in plain view, next to the shriveled apple.

"I'd like to buy back the watercolors," I said. "Ten dollars, wasn't it?"

"Oh, no," he replied. "They're much more than that now."

"How much, then, twenty, fifty, a hundred?" I pulled out my wallet and started counting out twenties. "I'm out of work now, so I can't afford too much. But I need those paints."

"We don't want your money, Mr. Stauf. At this stage, we like to deal in things that are far more abstract–and permanent. If you take the paints again, they will be a part of you from now on. Do you understand what I am saying?"

"What's there to understand?" I asked. "I'll do whatever it takes to get back those paints. They're part of my calling in life."

"We know," he said. "We're the ones that did the calling."

.   .   .   .   .   .

As I stood outside The Last One Standing with the Thanadiem paints under my arm, I was nagged by a sense that I had left something important in the shop, but after a moment or two I stopped trying to remember what it was. I breathed in the air of April. It was spring, the start of new life for someone, but it just as easily could be the end for somebody else. For me it was a good time to get on with my career, expand upon my calling.

I pulled from my wallet the picture of Detective Armstrong. It was a bit wrinkled, but I could still make out the features that made him look like the guy on the Smith Brothers Cough Drop box, the full beard and the curly hair, but also the features that distinguished him personally, the definite furrows in his forehead and the tight clothes.

It would do.

02
The Attic

Spring fever, clutter attacks, the need to create space for a new car in the previously completely filled garage–there are innumerable motivations for throwing out unwanted items. Maybe someone feels guilty after hearing George Carlin's diatribe on all the "stuff" we accumulate, even to the point that we need to rent storage units.

For me it was, "Dear, we need to scrape together some items for the community drive to raise money for the new park. The yard sale is next weekend. The money raised will go for new equipment."

"But didn't we give away everything we could spare for last year's drive?" I asked, hoping to avoid the time-consuming task that usually meant giving away several items I'd rather keep.

"There's plenty more. Besides, I'm in charge of the yard sale, and it wouldn't look good if we didn't show up with some contributions. Have you thought about donating some of your old paintings? They might fetch a decent amount."

"Forget that," I said, in a voice that betokened defensiveness built upon years of paranoia that my family didn't really appreciate my art.

"Well, then, how about the attic? We haven't really explored it in years. Surely, there is something in it we can part with."

"I'll see," I mumbled, though the thought of ascending the pull down ladder to reach the attic and then breathing air saturated with particles of Owens Corning insulation didn't particularly inspire me.

"Today is Tuesday. You'd better do it now because I need to deliver it all by Thursday."

Soon, I found myself standing in the hall, staring up at a rectangular piece of plywood, painted the same color as the rest of the ceiling, with a six-inch piece of cord dangling down, a knot in its lower end. I pulled on the cord and was greeted by a loud groaning as the springs expanded, exposing a tri-folded set of stairs, each hinged to the next. I also received a shower of dust and debris, plus a wave of stale air, convincing me that at least four or five years had elapsed since I last opened this door.

After climbing the rickety ladder and stepping on to one of the several four by eight plywood boards that served as a floor over the ceiling joists, I located a light—a single 60 watt bulb hanging from a cord—and began my survey of the purgatory of possessions filling the attic space, items that through no real fault of their own were never to reenter my family's world, doomed by their condition (mainly being out of style, though size played a part) or possible loss of utility to forever remain hidden away, but not thrown away.

The closest item (and no doubt the last to arrive) was a lamp, with a beige shade that I suspected looked dusty even before we bought it. It could go to the yard sale.

Behind the lamp an oval rug lay draped across (and partially obscuring) a morose burgundy colored chest of drawers, with brass handles. The rug was either too small or too large for any floor space in the house, or perhaps it was too faded or stained, but judging by its interwoven stripes of orange, green, and purple, I'm sure it was damned to the attic for its ugliness. The same was true of the chest of drawers. Both were fair game for the yard sale.

In a limbo off to the right stood a collection of children's toys, including a rocking horse, with leather strips for a mane, a red wagon, a doll house with a wooden family sitting together in the living room, a canister of Lincoln Logs, a child-sized guitar, all considered to be archaic by children who had grown up and moved on. I thought about adding them to the yard sale inventory, but I still held on to the possibility that they could be passed on to grandchildren, should there be any.

Close to the toys were cardboard boxes filled with books we were sure we would read or reread—*Moby Dick*, *The Sound and the Fury*, *Henderson the Rain King*, for instance. The odds were slim of their ever again actually resting in our hands–given all the electronic means to read books. Send them to the yard sale.

Stacked behind the boxes of books were sealed plastic containers, filled with sweaters, scarves, and mittens made out of wool. I wondered if the very fact that they were woolens doomed them to this outland, being scratchy and now replaceable by softer fabrics, including smart wools, which keep a body just as warm. I decided they could go. I knew I would probably never wear any of them again unless the ice age returned suddenly.

Behind the boxes was a contraption that could have only been stolen from a hotel–or bought at some other yard sale. It was designed for hanging clothes–and rolling them about. Visions of a bell-hop whisked through my mind. It consisted of two three-foot bars on the bottom with four wheels, two upright bars approximately five feet high, and a crossing bar about six feet long, from which hung an array of skirts, dresses, blouses, pants, shirts, and sport coats. It didn't take too much thought to figure out why they were in the attic: either style or weight gain.

How is it possible that a garment could be a favorite one day and seem so hopelessly wrong the next? And how could rational people fool themselves into thinking they would ever slim down enough to fit into these relics of the past? The whole collection could be donated for the yard sale, and I'd throw in the clothes rack if I could figure out how to get it out of the attic.

Appropriately positioned near the clothes rack rested a shoe rack, containing a wide assortment of women's, men's, and children's shoes– in a variety of styles, including wingtips, loafers, work boots, golf shoes, high heels, higher heels, children's tennis shoes in a rainbow of colors– all outgrown or rejected for style. They could all go to help the park.

In yet another area sat electronics/electrical appliances, all of which, though no doubt still serviceable, had been replaced by the new boys in town. These included VCR's, a Brother word processor, a Remington typewriter, a couple of rotary telephones, various electronic games, and an upright vacuum (which, as I remember, was simply too loud). Clumped together, with the vacuum in the middle, they reminded me of a comic book transformer. What a surprise some buyer at the yard sale would get if all that pile of electrical paraphernalia turned into a killing machine.

I also spotted some old golf clubs and an undersized golf bag, long since replaced by modern oversized equipment, which, unfortunately, did little to improve my game, but which certainly looked good on the back of a cart, the bag being too big for me to tote on foot around a golf course. Maybe a walker would buy my old clubs at the yard sale. I'd throw in the golf shoes sitting on the shoe rack.

Taking up lots of space behind me was a regular double-bed head board with side rails. It had been replaced downstairs by queen-sized furnishings, or, in one case, a king-sized bed, with the penalty that I was never quite sure that anyone was in bed with me. I was surprised not to find a mattress and box springs. Maybe we'd given them away already. At least they were gone now, thus allowing me to avoid a struggle to get them down for the yard sale.

Neatly stacked next to the head board and rails was a set of suitcases, the kind one sees only in old movies, sufficiently large to carry half of one's belongings across the ocean to London or Paris or wherever. Rising fees on checked baggage now made them obsolete. Plus, it would take a much younger man than I to lift them, when packed, even from the car to the curb at the airport. I glowed at the thought of the extra space that would be available with the removal of just the bed equipment and the suitcases.

Up to this point, I was actually enjoying myself, thinking about all the free space that would be available now, ostensibly to fill with more discards still enjoying some currency in the lives of us residing below: electric alarm clocks, a toaster oven, digital phones that still required plugging into an outlet, shoes and clothes that were still in style and still fit, but had become too boring to wear.

But my next discovery changed my mood.

It came when I looked behind the chest of drawers and spotted several paintings leaning against the back of it. I picked up two of them and carried them out nearer to the light bulb so I could see them better. They were two of my older paintings, ones that had hung for years in the living room. I couldn't even remember when they were taken down and brought to the attic, perhaps because I was working on some new paintings or, more likely, because they were lost works even when they were on the walls, with no one ever commenting on them. It was as if they had become a part of the walls, like a mirror or family photographs. I remember being thrilled when an electrician, who had come to the house to install a new outlet, told me how much he liked a painting I had done of a barn, which was hanging in the dining room. Even when I hung some of my new works, no one in my family ever commented on them, unless I specifically asked, "How do you like my new cabin painting?" which usually elicited a bland comment, such as "It's nice."

I didn't fare much better when I gave them one of my works, which prompted an equally ungratifying response, such as "I wonder where we can hang it." How I longed for just one comment about a particular aspect of any of my paintings, even a negative criticism, something to indicate that they had studied the form, color, subject—anything. The irony of it all was that they really wanted to keep the ones I gave them, as I learned when I asked if I could hang one of them at my own house. My request was met by vociferous protests about its being their favorite.

I brought out into the light several more paintings. They were all ones that I had done over the years, usually with subjects meaningful to the family or related to the locale in which we lived, but which had received no comments beyond the holistic summaries the others had received and which were now no more remembered than the oversized suitcases or the clothes rack. Whatever was to become of them, they were definitely not going to any yard sale.

There were still three paintings leaning against the chest, so I gathered them and returned to the light. To my surprise they were three paintings my mother had done and which had hung in her house during all the years of my growing up there.

The first one was an oil, approximately 24 by 30 inches, featuring a ship at sea, which was leaning to port as if a particularly powerful wave had hit it broadside. It was a three-master with the sails divided evenly between those that were up billowing in the wind and those that were roped down. Despite the tilted position, it looked strong and resilient, surrounded by a dark blue sea. Complementing the blue of the sea and the whitecaps was a sky that was a lighter blue, streaked across by white and orange clouds that blocked the late afternoon sun, giving the painting a kind of glow, even a hint of a magical aura. I could imagine that being on that ship would create a combination of fear, exhilaration, and peace.

The second one was a narrow rectangle, perhaps 14" tall by 30" wide, also an oil, a seascape with waves crashing onto a boulder-strewn shore, with the rocks curving to the left and away from the beach, forming a kind of jetty. There were four or five waves—at different heights, rolling toward the rocks. Their tops changed from whitecaps to splashing surf as they hit the rocks, making most of the bottom third of the painting a study in white. In the distance, rising out of the sea, lay a mountainous island, which was colored a bluish-purple. Hovering above the sea, out beyond the breakers, hung four seagulls, seemingly suspended by another kind of magical force. I could practically hear them, as well as the whoosh and crash of the waves hitting the rocks, and I could feel the spray sweeping over me.

The third, a pastel, was also rectangular, but vertical, being approximately 14" wide and 30" tall. It pictured a house encircled by a small stream. A path ran from the house down to the stream, and another continued up from the stream on the near side bank. There were several trees surrounding the house, with two tall, spindly ones with a dearth of foliage dominating the scene. The house itself, mostly white, was basically square, but bore a dormer side extension. A chimney sat on top. The creek was colored the hues of the surrounding scenes—with a mixture of green, yellow, and brown, streaked to give the illusion of motion.

All three had dates on them indicating that she painted them when she about twenty years old. If I were to classify her works, I'd have to take into account the ethereal quality in all three paintings and the hint of wildness in each and label her as a romantic, a term I would have been hard pressed to use for her, given her generally conservative lifestyle. Maybe she was a different person when she was twenty, or maybe the process of painting made her different.

They hung in our house every day as I grew up, but I never took the time to ask about them, though she probably needed as much reinforcement and feed back as I do now. Then for several years after she died and I inherited them at her bequest, I hung them in prominent places in my house—mostly as decoration because at the time, having not actually begun my own career as an artist, I had lots of bare walls. I can't recall who moved them to the attic or when, but I also don't remember raising any objections over their deportation.

I didn't know if more of her paintings existed. Probably, they did.. Had she given them away to people she believed would appreciate them? Were they stored in someone's attic at that very moment? Did they have romantic themes?

These were only a couple of the questions that arose as I studied the three that were mine. What were the models or inspiration for each one? Had she sat on the shore to paint the one with rocks and surf? Was it a real place? Where was it? Obviously she could not have been on site for the ship painting, but did she simply make up the scene or had she seen some other rendition that she emulated? Whose house was in the third painting? What kind of trees did she try to represent? Why did she turn to pastels after doing oils, or did she start out with pastels?

I came to understand the character of Emily at the end of Thornton Wilder's *Our Town*, who, buried in the cemetery, speaks to the audience. She wishes she could have one day to go back to be with her family and say and ask things she failed to while she was alive. I longed to tell my mother how much I liked her paintings, to ask her the questions that were in my mind right then, to let her know how much her paintings, even though I had not discussed them with her, had influenced me in my own art work. How nice it would have been for our two artistic worlds to overlap, even for a day.

I wondered if taking things for granted was a genetic trait that I had passed on to my children, or had I somehow engrained in them an apathy toward art done by family members. After all, I had not directed their attention to Mother's work. Could I really blame them for treating my paintings with the same indifference?

What could I do to atone for my failure? I started by taking Mother's three paintings down the ladder and finding a cloth to rid them of the dust that had accumulated on them. Then I surveyed the walls of my house, searching for the best place for each one. My wife appeared as I was doing the latter, saying, "Oh good, you've found some art to give to the yard sale. There's plenty more somewhere around here."

"On the contrary," I replied, "these need a prominent place here in our house. Mother painted them." She must have sensed my resolve and stayed out of the process as I replaced some family photos, all of which included relatives I never cared for. And I vowed that when any of my children visited, I would draw their attention to the three paintings, pointing out details.

Then I turned my attention to my own art work. After clearing out most of what remained in the attic (leaving the children's toys), I made a low-budget art gallery, where I hung my pieces. Is it egotistical to admire your own art? I don't think so, especially if you're the only one. I took to heart a line from Erasmus's *The Praise of Folly*, "So what if the world hisses at you, as long as you applaud yourself."

But in the back of my mind I hoped for a day when one of my children came to the attic to either deposit some junk, retrieve one of the toys from his own childhood, or clear out whatever was in there—and in the process discovered my art—and had the same epiphany that I had when I found Mother's art. I hoped he would ask questions about purpose, shape, medium, etc. It would be nice if I were still alive to answer some of the questions, but I could rest easier in my grave if a child of mine had a true artistic attic experience.

Anything, as long as he didn't give my paintings away to a yard sale.

03
The Silhouette

There was nothing about the picture that would make me want to keep it. It was a life-sized silhouette, with a side view of the neck and head of a boy, probably around six or seven. The head was a cut-out of black paper mounted on a stained and faded white background. The mat around it was also black and likewise looked the worse for wear.

The frame was another matter. It was cut to accommodate a standard 16 x 20 matted picture; it was attractive, a medium dark walnut; it was in good condition, with no discernible nicks or dents; and it was flat, about two inches wide on all four sides. I had become choosey about frames, avoiding those with a beveled back, since the latter made difficult the process of sealing them with paper. The glass was a bonus, being, though dirty, unscratched and unchipped. A little Windex would make it quite serviceable.

"How much for this one?" I asked, handing the picture to Bob, the owner of the thrift store I was in.

"I need to get five dollars for it. That frame is made of walnut."

"Fine, I'll take it," which must have surprised him since I normally haggled with him. I'm not cheap, but I do like a bargain, especially if it has anything to do with art supplies.

"Need a bag?" he asked, reaching for a pile of plastic sacks that previously served customers at Walmart or one of many local grocery stores.

"Nope, I'll take it as is." With that, I paid the price and then left the store, a privately owned business that sold a combination of true antiques, reusable goods, and undisguised junk. It was one of several thrift stores I frequented, including those sponsored by well known chains, such as The Salvation Army, Habitat for Humanity, and Goodwill, those serving as hospital and library auxiliaries, and local businesses like this one, Bob's Nearly New Shoppe, whose name bothered me in that "Bob's" and "Shoppe" didn't seem to go together any more than would "Bob's" and "First National Bank."

I typically scavenged for frames, hoping they still had glass. I really did not care what the pictures were. Most of them were cheap reprints of famous, or unfamous, paintings, so I usually discarded them when I got around to using the frames and/or glass. I rarely stumbled across any picture worth keeping. I was sure the proprietor would have snared anything valuable when it first came in, or one of several customers who got there ahead of me could have hit it lucky.

I liked Bob's because it was generally well organized, with the usual sections of books and magazines, clothes and shoes, small appliances, furniture that didn't take up too much room, such as hassocks, table lamps, and small chairs, electronics that probably no longer worked, toys, and tools. Paintings, photographs, bare frames, and picture frame glass were all together in one section in the back corner. I had endured my share of accidents in thrift stores that were cluttered, once catching my foot in a vacuum cleaner cord protruding into the aisle and taking a nose dive into a laundry basket filled with old cassette tapes. Bob kept his aisles clear, which made it easier to go directly to the pictures.

My wife once asked me, "When you're in the thrift shops, do you ever look at anything other than frames?"

I replied, "No, because all the older goods remind me of what I don't have in my possession as remnants of my past." She already knew about how I lost my parents some twenty years earlier, when I was six, and being raised by a martinet/aunt who had little tolerance for any items in the house with sentimental value.

When I arrived home, I put the framed silhouette in my art supply storeroom, where I keep my stock of frames bought at thrift stores in one section and new frames I bought in conventional art supply stores in another.

Over the next few months I stayed busy painting, Several times I was tempted to use the walnut frame, but it was never quite right for what I had painted, including a watercolor of a dilapidated barn, an oil of an old wheelbarrow, and another watercolor of a ramshackle beach house, all of which were too rustic to match the smooth formality of the frame. I at first thought it would go well with a painting I finished of some daffodils growing around a stump, but it was just a bit too dark.

Each time I considered the frame, instead of discarding the picture in it, I studied the silhouetted figure a little more. He had a bowl-cut hair style, medium height forehead, eyebrows that protruded just slightly, a semi-pointed nose, non-protruding lips, and a small neck, on which the head sat, slightly tilted forward. Having no children of my own, I could not judge for sure the demeanor of the boy, but somehow, perhaps due to the medium, he appeared to be gentle and kind. He obviously had been the child of someone who valued him, as evidenced by the effort to have the silhouette done, which more often than not was a costly process, usually involving a professional.

It was not long before I began to carry the silhouetted shape around in my head when I was out and about doing chores unrelated to my painting. I found myself looking carefully at any boy around the age of six or seven, especially any I saw in the area of Bob's "Shoppe," subconsciously hoping I would spot the real boy on whom the picture was based. I almost got into trouble a couple of times when, after gazing at boys for what must have been an unacceptable duration, I was accosted by some irate parents, one of whom called me "a sick pervert." I learned to be more discreet.

I finally traveled back to Bob's, taking with me the framed silhouette, the first visit I had made since my original purchase. "Do you happen to recall this picture I bought the last time I was in here?" I asked.

"Yep," he replied, "I remember charging you a little more for it because of the walnut frame. I probably could have gotten even more for it, maybe eight dollars, but I let you have it for five because you're a good customer."

"You don't also happen to remember who dropped it off, the person who owned it before it came here?"

"Can't recollect that. It's bound to have come in with a pile of other stuff, but as you know I separate the goods when I put them out for selling. There's no telling what else was with this picture. Could have been in a collection of stuff I bought at another thrift store that was folding. Isn't there a signature or date on it somewhere?"

"No, I'm afraid I'm out of luck there. Well, thanks."

I turned to go, but Bob spoke up again. "Mind if I ask why it's so important to find out about this particular piece? You've bought lots of pictures. What makes it so special?"

"I'm not sure I can tell you. Curiosity, I suppose." I didn't want him to think I was obsessed.

"Sorry I couldn't help you."

I returned home, but instead of placing the picture back in my store room, I set it on an easel in my studio. As I looked at the faded matting, I realized that several years must have passed since the piece was put together. I went immediately to my store room and searched through my stock for another work that had undergone approximately the same aging process. I knew I wasn't being very scientific, no carbon dating or anything like that, but I wanted at least a rough guess. I found three prints that had the same combination of glass, matting, and a picture on paper as did the silhouette, with approximately the same fading. Two of them had dates on them, one being twenty-one years ago, the other twenty-three.

I realized that if I were going to find the boy, whom I had named Tyler, I'd have to do some projecting, imagining what he would look like after some twenty years. So I began doing sketches of what I figured was the current version. I tried altering the facial features to make them look more mature, thickening the neck, changing the hair style, until I had a least a dozen versions of the boy grown older.

One benefit that evolved from the process was that I became more acutely aware of facial detail, such that I attempted some portrait paintings. Upon seeing them, my wife said, "That's unusual. You've not done faces before. Why now?"

"I guess I never had the confidence to deal up close and personal with people. It's probably another effect of my general lack of self worth that I've carried around with me since my parents died."

"Well, I certainly like you, and I especially dote on your face. Maybe you should do a self portrait."

"Thanks for the compliment. I'll consider it."

After settling on what I believed was the most accurate updating of the silhouette, I began scrutinizing any male adult approximately twenty-six years old, always keeping in mind that in the twenty years since the picture was constructed, Tyler could be seven states away. While trying to be more discreet than I had with boys, I would try to catch them in profile, which necessitated some awkward side stepping and shifting for position in some cases. No one called me a pervert, but I did get equally negative commentary, such as, "What the hell are you doing?" "Get away; I don't have any money to give you!" and "What are YOU looking at?" I did spot a few men who seemed to match the profile. In a couple of cases I engaged them in conversation, asking for directions so that I could see their faces from the side as they turned to point toward some location I asked about.

I persisted in my quest for months, but slowly my enthusiasm began to flag. I felt as if I had lost a son or at least a good friend. To pull myself out of my doldrums, I tried to paint some pictures, revisiting my favorite subjects—trees, barns, mountains, etc.—but nothing interested me, particularly portraits. I began to doubt my own abilities as an artist, almost thinking of myself as the failure my aunt had tried to make me believe I was.

Searching for any kind of inspiration, I pulled out a folder in which I kept a variety of pictures that had interested me, taken from magazines, postcards, and newspapers over the years. None of them awakened my languid muse.

It was while I was leafing through the folder that I came across three photographs, all of which had been taken since I went to live with my aunt: one of my aunt sitting on the steps of her house, frowning into the camera, another a picture of her, unsmiling, next to a car, and a third one of her and me, with her again glaring into the camera. I was about six or seven, and I was sitting next to her, turned to my right, looking at her. There were no pictures of my parents or of me when I was younger.

Several years before, I had retrieved the three pictures from a pile of household paraphernalia my aunt had gathered to throw away. Whenever I looked at them, my focus had always been on my aunt. Why was she so angry? Was it something I had done or said? What had been her relationship with my parents? Had she discarded pictures of my parents and me?

This time, however, I focused on the photograph that included me. There was something familiar about my face, in profile. I quickly retrieved the silhouette of Tyler and held it next to the photograph. The same haircut, the same slightly elongated forehead, the same hint of a pointed nose and protruding eyebrows and lips, the long, slender neck—they all matched. Was it possible that the silhouetted figure was me and that I had been searching for myself all along?

I wanted to think that it was, and even if I wasn't, the picture had opened doors for me that had long been closed. Among other things, I had new confidence that my parents would have thought enough of me to pay for a silhouette. Also, I had come to realize that I would like to have a child, a son or daughter that looked a bit like Tyler–or me. I had never been big on having children, again part of my lack of confidence, but that had changed. I wanted someone to whom I could pass on my art, someone I could take to the park, someone I could share an ice-cream with, someone I could make a silhouette for. If he turned out to be a boy, I'd name him Tyler. And now I felt confident about my artistic abilities. I was eager at that moment to begin painting again, particularly portraits.

There were lots of questions remaining about my past, but I didn't need answers anymore. I was satisfied. I hung the silhouette on the wall right in front of the desk at which I sat when painting. It would serve as my muse from then on.

Bob at the "Shoppe" was right. He should have charged me more.

04
Death of a Rival Artist

Though I've never been big on going to funerals–they give me the same uneasiness that I get on airplanes when the landing gear clunks down or the engines change cadence–I attended the one given for Bert Concade, a local artist, who died at the age of fifty-four. I went feeling an obligation to be a part of the artistic community that has lost one of its "family" members.

If there is such a thing as an art-related death, Burt had it. One of his large paintings, in a particularly heavy, ornate frame, broke loose from its mooring on the wall above him as he stooped to pick up a chunk of plaster he had dislodged when he drove an oversized nail into the wall to hang the picture. Apparently it hit him on the top of his head as if someone had delivered a blow with an ax.

The funeral took place in Backworth, South Carolina, at the First Methodist Church, whose very name made it sound more prestigious than the Second Methodist Church or any of several in town named after neighborhood roads. I was a bit puzzled that the service was not being held in an art gallery or museum, but maybe Concade was more religious than I had known.

by Joseph Meigs

According to the 5 x 7 program that I was given by a solemn-faced usher, whom I had seen at some of the art shows I attended, there was to be a preliminary viewing of the body in an open casket, followed by the meat of the service during which several fellow artists and friends would testify to Concade's worthiness as an artist and as a human being, I not having been asked to speak. The program was printed on yellow paper with green lettering (rage italics, I think), I suppose because those were his trademark colors, used to an excess in all his paintings.

I took a place in the line of body viewers, though I would have been perfectly content to skip this stage of the proceedings. He was lying on a slight incline in a dark green casket with a gold-colored velvet lining and gold-colored handles, dressed in a green suit and yellow shirt, thus taking into eternity the colors that had so often adorned his paintings. Behind the coffin, on easels, sat several of his paintings, chosen I suspected by the fact that they were dominated by yellows and greens. On a small table amidst the easels rested a photograph of Concade, which must have been taken at least twenty years previously, with him sporting more hair and a vibrant countenance, perhaps because the photo predated marriage and five children.

Concade himself in the coffin looked both better and worse than he had the last time I had seen him, at an art show in which we had been assigned ten by ten spaces right next to each other. The mortician had earned his pay by repairing–through the magic of facial paints and a putty that probably resembled the Bondo auto restorers use on a damaged car–what had to have been a sizeable dent in Concade's head, leaving him with a slightly furrowed brow, as if were unsure exactly where he was and what had happened to him. The mortician must have also sewn his lips shut, which made the occasion the first time I had ever heard Concade not talking.

What troubled me most was the waxy appearance the makeup gave Concade, making him look like a lacquered mannequin. I've always been under the impression that the mortician's ideal is to make a dead person look as if he is about to spring back into life, or, at worst, to appear to be sleeping. A line from Robert Browning's "My Last Duchess" popped into my head ("That's my last Duchess hanging on the wall / Looking as if she were alive."). Concade just looked dead, like a toy doll whose batteries had run down. Of course, lying in a coffin didn't do much to improve his appearance, even with gold-colored velvet lining.

After giving Concade one last viewing (in case he had given new meaning to the term "wake" and actually come back to life), I sat down on a pew in the sixth row and watched the other viewers. I recognized many of them from the art family, but there were several individuals who were strangers to me. Judging by their deferential attitude in approaching Concade, I suspected they were followers of his art, disciples hoping to get a glimpse of the man who had come to be known as the "Artist of Light."

Many of the viewers seemed uncomfortable walking in the slow moving procession, frequently stopping to glance at the people already seated, then, after discovering they had made a gap in the line, shuffling forward quickly as if they had been threatened with a cattle prod. Others, obviously trying to keep a slow but consistent pace, looked as if they were walking in ski boots. Several of them, when it became their turn to view the body, simply looked beyond the casket and studied Concade's paintings on the easels behind, rather than look directly at the body. I was betting that this was a first time experience for many of them to see Concade or his paintings.

I wondered if anyone in the procession disliked Concade as much as I did.

And why would anyone dislike Concade? Let me count the ways.

Putting his style of art aside for the moment, his artsy behavior bothered me as much as anything, and I can be a good witness on this score since some blind sadist managed to situate us next to each other at practically every show we both set up a booth for. He tried to dazzle artists and potential clients with volumes of pseudo-criticism of the arts in general and, specifically, the works done by other artists in our "family." He overpowered everyone as he pontificated about tonality and texture and the merits of broad stroke painting as opposed to small brush, or detailed, painting, which of course was totally ironic since most of his own paintings were done with the latter technique, with his usual overkill of yellows and greens, colors that he used as part of his sales pitch ("Ah, my dear, I see you are carrying a green purse and you have on yellow earrings. You're just the person my art was designed for. I bet you have a wall somewhere in your house, perhaps in your foyer, begging for a painting with these colors."). His favorite line was "I painted this just when the light was luminescent and radiant, making you feel that you are enveloped by that light." I would have given anything to have a booth–any booth, even one selling strings of beads or home-made pencil sharpeners–between us.

As if being a next door party to all of his persuasions weren't enough, I had to endure his frequent visits to my booth to report a sale or to check out my sales. It was if we were in competition, which I guess we were. To make matters even worse, each time he sold a work, he would make a grand display of replacing it. "Would you watch my booth while I run to my van?" he would ask. "I don't want to miss another sale while I'm gone." Then he would make a big production of bringing back the replacement, swinging by my booth once again to show me the new one, a smirk on his face. "Thanks, I'll take over now," he would say. I hated to tell him, but I had not given his booth a moment's thought while he was gone.

I had visions of grabbing the painting and whacking him over the head with it, leaving him with his head poking up through the torn canvas, looking like a dog wearing one of those cone shaped devices its vet recommended to keep it from scratching its face or ears.

Of course, it goes without saying that his clothes always matched his behavior, usually including a foppish scarf wrapped once around his neck, even in warm weather, a black beret, and a pipe, which drooped, unlit, from his lips at every art show, but nowhere else. He used it to point at a particular part of a painting he was trying to sell.

The blind sadist that juxtaposed us at art shows must have steered us both at the same time to visit the men's room, where Concade used the opportunity of a captive audience to further his theories on art. I learned the technique of a "quick pee," which meant I had to return to the men's room not long after the first visit, but without his presence. I'm surprised he didn't try to recommend Flo-Max to me.

After the last viewer had been seated, the Concade family, led by his widow and five children, made its entrance, filling the first four rows on each side of the aisle. Judging by the number, Concade must have had scores of siblings, in-laws, parents, grandparents, uncles, aunts, nieces, nephews, etc. The only ones I recognized were Mrs. Concade and the oldest son, who had occasionally helped his father set up an art booth. Mrs. Concade seemed more miffed than sorrowful, making me wonder if she were angry at God for prematurely calling home one of her family members, angry at her husband for leaving her with so many children or for leaving her with a skimpy death benefit, or angry at the rest of us in the "artists community" for somehow not protecting him from killer frames.

Once they were all settled in, we were treated to some music befitting Concade's emphasis on brightness and light, including "You Are My Sunshine," "Sunshine on My Shoulders," and "Ain't No Sunshine When You're Gone." Being a fan of the movie *The Big Chill*, I was kind of disappointed that "Jeremiah Was a Bull Frog" wasn't included.

Then a string of "testifiers" took turns, praising Concade for his civic involvement (which included being a Boy Scout leader, a member of the NRA, a blood donor, and president of the county art council, a position I thought I should have had), his accomplishments as an artist (various prizes and a questionable inclusion in an annual of *Who's Who Among Artists in South Carolina*, a volume that Concade had to pay $78 to receive), and his influence on other artists with his bright, garish style. I began to drift a bit, but I did pick up some laudations that included "We have truly lost a ray of light. Just like the light, his spirit surrounds us even now," asserted by Antonio McGirtz, a particularly ardent disciple

by Joseph Meigs

of Concade. "He truly was the master of light, who taught us a new appreciation of yellow and green," another zealous supporter exclaimed, adding that "Whenever we see yellows and greens—in trees, flowers, art—we'll be reminded of him." I wondered if I would think of Concade every time I pulled up to a traffic light or every time I saw a John Deere tractor.

No one mentioned his pedantry or overbearing and obnoxious competiveness with other artists.

After the service I stood in line to offer my condolences to the family, particularly to Mrs. Concade, who went by Dorothy. Everyone spoke to her in hushed tones, usually giving her a hug befitting a funeral—not an air hug, but certainly not a grab-em and hold-em type. As I shuffled forward, I listened to the comments and conversations of those closest to me in line: "I saw him just days ago. You can never tell what's going to happen in life." "How old was he? I think he was younger than I am." "Who will ever fill the gap of great art he's leaving behind?" "Who will take over as President of the Art Council?" "I wish the line would move faster; I'm missing my afternoon nap."

When I finally stood before Dorothy, she glared at me and said, "I'm surprised you came. Burt always knew how you felt about his art. So did I. It was hard missing it in the reviews in which you so mercilessly panned his art." I contemplated giving her a hug, but her body language suggested otherwise. So I muttered, "Believe me," citing a line from Tolstoy's "The Death of Ivan Ilyich" (the translated version obviously). Then, realizing that was not enough, I added, "He was part of the art community. We have to support each other. I'm sure he would have come to my funeral."

She looked at me hard, as if she were going to say, "I doubt it," but then swung her attention to the next person in line, leaving me to sign off with another "Believe me."

Feeling an intense need to get out of there, I exited as quickly as I could, pushing my way through the crowd, even skipping the finger food that had been set out (for what? To reward those who came to a funeral?

To encourage the art community to "break bread together"?). Despite Mrs. Concade's blatant hostility toward me, I felt satisfied that I had done my part to support the artistic community.

We are like a family, you know.

05
The Hungry Artist
A Kafkan Clone

Is it true that there is no difference between the artist and his art? Does an artist's sense of self-worth depend upon the public's reception or rejection of his work?

These are questions that I, Gregory Sampson, have been forced to consider since, during the last few years, the public's interest in paintings by local artists has slackened alarmingly, particularly works sold at arts and crafts shows. I should know; I'm one of those local artists.

It used to be that wall art dominated the sales over crafts, but now patrons turn their eyes to the bricks and mortar of a utilitarian life—items for them to drink from or eat off of or to use while feeding dogs, cats, squirrels, and birds. Or they simply cut to the chase and buy food they themselves can gobble down immediately.

There was a time when I could depend on practically the whole community turning out for a show, keeping me and the other artists busy all day long, inspecting all of the works in the booths. They would ask such questions as "Did you paint on site or from a photograph?" or "What inspired you for that particular detail?" and then offer compliments about tonality, texture, composition, or color, all leading to a great number of purchases. Patrons, often as many as seven or eight, crowded together in my ten-by-ten booth, would argue over who had priority and bicker over purchasing rights, shouting, "I was here first!" or "I asked about that painting before anyone else!" This was especially true with people who knew me personally, who apparently believed they were entitled to my art through acquaintance. In all cases, I proudly signed the purchased piece on the back and put down the current date and then attached one of my business cards, which were sought after since each one had a tiny reprint of one of my paintings.

I could particularly count on selling all of the originals I brought to the show, and if by some quirk I was able, during the day of the show, to paint a new piece, it was usually sold before I even finished it. Plus, there was always a strong market for the reproductions I brought to the show, either shrink-wrapped or framed. And extending my sales even farther, I often was hired to do a commissioned painting of someone's barn or house. Of course, having a prime spot assigned to me helped my sales also.

Parents would bring their children to my booth and say, "This man, dressed all in black, is a real artist. He painted all of these pictures. Maybe some day you'll be like him and paint too," whereupon the children would look at me in awe, even holding tightly to each other's hands for security, as if they were in the presence of the mighty Oz. Sometimes a child or his parent would ask if I would permit the touching of my hand, as if such an act might convey magical artistic powers. I always was willing to oblige.

I stayed so busy that eventually I was forced to hire an assistant, who would help take the patrons' money and wrap the purchased paintings using the paper I had bought from a butcher's shop. He would also help me keep the booth clean and neat, picking up litter left by some overly eager looker, straighten the pictures that were knocked askew by one of those crowded inside, make sure all my price tags and name cards for the paintings as well as my sign that read "Welcome to my mini-gallery"– had not fallen on the ground, and record all my sales in a ledger I brought to every show. He would also assist in serving food to the visitors: mints, veggies with dips, crackers and cheese, and, from time to time, petit fours. On more than one occasion I was accused of bribing people to buy my art by feeding them, but I only intended to make the experience of seeing my art as pleasant as possible.

I myself rarely had spare time during a show, so I endured a self-imposed artist's version of a fast, one that I extended from show to show such that eventually I would be nauseated if I tried to eat while a show was in progress. But I was never hungry during the fairs since I was filled with an elation that comes from being respected.

At the end of each show day, the visitors would often demand that I and the other artists stay open past the announced closing hour, even asking for lights to be shone on the booths, in order for the crowds to see as many of the works as possible. I personally kept two or three flashlights handy for these occasions. Eventually the show organizers would need to come around and remind the artists and the patrons that it was well past time to close down.

If the show ran more than one day, many of the first-day customers would return on subsequent days and buy a second or third or even fourth work. These were the salad days of artistic appreciation, and I, along with the other artists, basked in adulation and sales. I was even glad when other artists were selling well, believing that I was part of a community of artists and also believing in the notion of art for art's sake, especially if that art was in a form that I admired and respected, including paintings, photography, woodworking, basketry, fabric and fiber arts (including quilting and weaving), glass blowing, and pottery. This sense of community manifested itself at the end of many shows, when several of us artists would trade pieces of near-equal value. I amassed quite a collection of other artists' works through these means.

Things went so well that I didn't even mind the arduous process of setting up and tearing down. In order to avoid an extra trip, and thus save on expenses for gasoline, I usually chose to set up my booth early on the first morning of the show, arriving three hours early if it was outside, two and a half hours early if indoors, sometimes leaving my house at three or four in the morning in order to give myself ample time to set up. It made for some extremely busy days, but I endured the difficulty because I loved offering my art to the public.

An outdoor show was more difficult, of course, since it entailed setting up a tent, with zip-up side panels and some kind of tarp on the ground, along with awnings extending out at the top to protect the paintings near the outer edges of the booth. Even a hint of rain complicated matters when the show was outdoors, since the paper backing on the paintings tended to absorb moisture from the air and began to crinkle. A hard rain, if accompanied by strong winds, necessitated returning all the paintings to the seven or eight large plastic tubs I used for transporting works to and from the shows. In these circumstances, I simply had to wait out the storm, hoping it would pass quickly and leave me time to re-hang all the paintings before the day ended. Rain was a doubly negative factor since it had the potential to ruin my paintings and since it did, in fact, keep people from visiting my booth, while the sides hung down for protection.

Rain or shine, indoors or outdoors, I still had to unload from my truck a number of display boards, easels, tables, in addition to the plastic tubs. Of course, at the end of the show, I had to reverse the process.

And there was always the matter of a non-refundable entry fee, which could be quite dear for some shows, but I did not mind paying it since I usually sold lots of paintings.

The only other negative I experienced came occasionally from the organizers, who seemed to watch me carefully to make sure, I suspect, that I actually was selling my own works, and did not, on the sly, substitute in paintings imported from China, which I might have bought out of a large truck in a parking lot on a weekend.

At the end of each day, I felt the fatigue of a dock worker or a package loader for UPS, suffering leg cramps and an achy back, but the pain was ameliorated by a sense of accomplishment, plus I often had the privilege during the day to listen to a wide variety of nearby entertaining musicians, some of whom sang golden oldies, while others offered country. I don't remember ever hearing hard rock or heavy metal at the shows.

If the show was outside, I also had the chance to see, and often pet, a menagerie of dogs, ranging from purebreds to multi-mixed composites, all of them leading their owners around by leashes that sometimes were larger than the dogs themselves.

But something has changed. We live in a different world today Very few people buy my art now at the shows, and it's not because they are buying from my artistic competitors, who have fallen on bad times just as I have.

Maybe it has been caused by the economic decline sweeping the country, and people simply have less money to spend. Maybe it is due to the influx into the beautiful area in which I live—and where I have most of my shows—of outsiders from states that do not encourage an appreciation of art. Maybe the lack of funding for the arts in public schools has taken its toll, or maybe the proliferation of electronic gadgetry—cell phones, i-pods, blackberries, text messaging, twittering, etc.—has killed off much of the desire to see and experience original art on display.

Whatever the cause, my sales have steadily declined, even among my friends and among those who request commissioned paintings. Fewer and fewer visitors come to my tent, to the point that I have been forced to let go my assistant and give up serving food to the customers.

And it seems to me that those who do come by are ruder and more distant than customers in the past. I now notice disrespectful behavior that I was unaware of before when sales were flourishing. Maybe this behavior was there all along and I was too busy to notice, but I don't think so.

I have learned not to be offended by the people who walk past my booth without even looking at me, signifying a total absence of interest in my art, or, for that matter, the arts in general. I have to admit that I myself tend not to look closely at a booth filled with what I consider to be knick knacks, so how can I legitimately blame anyone for not liking my particular art.

No, the people who make me feel small actually do look at my booth, but only from the safety of ten feet out. They of course see only the paintings mounted on the front display panels. Maybe they figure the place is under quarantine.

They must be the more timid cousins of those who come to the opening of the booth, but who refuse to step over the imaginary boundary, keeping their feet planted outside, but leaning over into the tent with their upper torsos to the maximum degree before toppling over. I wonder if they have seen too many horror movies wherein there is always some line between good and evil—the threshold of a house, railroad tracks, a disreputable street, or a river such as the Styx—and they considered it sinful to step into my den of iniquity. Many of them simply point at works from outside, making me wonder if they have an ancestry of hunting dogs.

At least these people, as well as the lazy oafs who use the front and rear openings of my tent as a shortcut, don't take up too much of my time. But there are plenty who do.

Included in this group are those who do actually stop by the booth, make glowing comments about the beauty of the paintings, but, unlike my customers of old who were eager to buy a work, seem to have a ready-made excuse for why they can't purchase any of them.

They say, "I'd love to buy one of these, but my walls are completely covered with family photos and some paintings I picked up a few years ago." I can readily imagine prints bought at big box stores or faded photographs of family members. In the latter case I'm tempted to say, "Why don't you give Aunt Mildred a rest. Hasn't she been hanging too long?"

Or they act as if they are totally unaware of their living accommodations and say, "I'll have to check our house for space and color before we buy."

If they are truly that unobservant, I don't want one of my works in their house.

Some people, after studying my paintings and asking questions, avoid purchasing a work by saying they did not bring any cash, a checkbook, or a credit card with them to the show. They often precede this declaration by frisking themselves with full body patting as if they are searching for a way to pay, or locate a weapon

I wonder what they might do in an emergency demanding payment to a tow truck driver or tire repairman or how they are going to pay for the snacks I am certain they are going to get from a food vendor.

Unlike my customers of old who trusted my sense of coordination enough that they bought my paintings exactly as I had matted and framed them, some of the new breed claim that they might buy a particular painting if only it had been mounted in a different colored frame. They share a kinship with the patrons who, after looking at every painting I have on display, ask if I have any pictures of something I obviously have NOT painted: a cow, pig, bear, moose, goose, fox, or outhouse, for example. After I tell them no, they usually hang around for a few minutes explaining why they are fond of a particular animal or building. And if I suddenly remember that I in fact have hidden away a picture of what they have requested, say an outhouse, their response is something along the lines of, "But I need a painting of THREE outhouses together." In such a scenario, I am tempted to go that extra step and claim that I DO have a painting with three outhouses to see what their response would be. But actually I don't want to hear any more from these people. They're as boring as a church bulletin.

Much of my time is spent listening to visitors who look at my works and then proclaim to a companion, "Madge, you could paint something like this one." I would like to jump in and ask, "Madge, when was the last time you painted anything, and what are the odds you will ever paint something like this?" and then add to the first speaker, "If you like it, buy it; just don't delude yourself into thinking Madge or any of your other friends will do one like it."

I could give similar advice to the people who look at a scene I've done, let's say a road, and then proclaim, "Why that looks just like the one on my property," as if that's a reason NOT to buy the painting.

Among the most disrespectful visitors are those who leave my booth in a mess, either by tossing litter on the ground, by knocking my works about, or by touching everything. I can almost tolerate children who put their cotton-candied fingers on the glass of a painting, but I really can't abide adults who do it, usually as they point out to a companion (or even to themselves) a limb or bird or anything specific in a painting. They are related to the customers who have to pick up a painting, as if measuring its heft as part of their deliberations about worth. They in turn must be related to the people who, when deciding whether to buy a book in a bookstore, have to hold it and flip through the pages. They all probably kick the tires of cars they're thinking of purchasing. Whomever they are related to, I end up using a lot of Windex after they leave.

I'm also not too keen on the people who demean my work by attempting to bargain with me. "You're going to cut me a deal, aren't you?" asks a buyer from a big city in Florida, to whom I have already quoted the lowest price I can offer and still make any profit. "I bet you don't want to have to pack up any more of these than necessary," says a man in Bermuda shorts and black socks, "so how about giving me one of these at half price." I've decided that I'd rather not make any sale if it means lowering the price–and thus the worth—of my paintings.

The people who insult me the most are those that buy junky crafts at the show rather than art. They show up at my tent with bags filled with the stuff I would most likely NOT buy myself. Tim O'Brien wrote a story called "The Things They Carried" about the objects soldiers in Vietnam kept in their pockets or hauled around on their backs. I could write a story about the things that the new wave of shoppers at arts and crafts shows tote from booth to booth and call it "The Crap They Carried." Here's a sample: wooden boards with folksy adages painted on or burned into having to do with the roles played in life by men and women or the advantages of living in a particular town; soap labeled as"Forest Pine" but smelling more like Pinesol Cleaner; "natural" looking ceramic ornaments (deer, herons, bears, bunnies, chickens, etc., particularly in pairs); rocks with candles implanted in them (matching exactly what in nature I've never been clear about); jewelry (like the baubles the Yahoos in *Gulliver's Travels* wore); weapons of minor destruction (rubber bands and clothespins are usually involved); potpourri in cellophane bags; religious figurines (saints, praying hands, Jesus in Gethsemane); clanky wind chimes; Santa Claus and/or Mrs. Claus and/or elves made from clothes pins, light bulbs, or popsicle sticks; hero and heroine actions figures, taken from the pages of comic books and carved out of vegetables; and "functional" crafts, such as an apparatus with corn cobs mounted on the ends of two crossing narrow boards that supposedly lure squirrels to grab on and then swing about until they are too dizzy to eat your birdseed.

Most of this is stuff that buyers keep around for about three days after the purchase and then relegate to a deep drawer or discard altogether. It must have been the kind of stuff the Sundance Kid had in mind when Butch Cassidy, after the two of them along with Etta Place had just disembarked from a train in Bolivia, said, "You get a lot for your money in Bolivia. I checked on it." Sundance's response was, "What could they have here that you would possibly want to buy?"

These people all are in league with those who come to an arts and crafts show for the sole purpose of finding food, in this case, in its worst forms, such as butter-soaked popcorn (in bags big enough to store all the leaves raked from one's yard in late fall); a combination called Indian fry bread (with "fry" being the most important word); pork rinds (fried fat); gooey candied whatevers; and a staple at outdoor shows: cotton candy. They buy this stuff because supposedly they don't normally get it at home, but I'm quite sure it wouldn't matter if the food vendors served ordinary fare, such as plain sugar cookies or peanut butter sandwiches. If it's food or junky crafts, there are always going to be buyers.

I could tolerate these people better if much of what they intended to eat didn't end up my paintings and if the vendors selling it all were not ever located next to me, since the patrons often line up for their booths in front of mine, blocking my entry.

These buyers, more so than the craftsmen and vendors who offer such stuff, are the ones that if I were the narrator named Montressor in Edgar Allan Poe's "The Cask of Amontillado," I would lure them with an expensive amontillado, or a recently discovered piece by a celebrated artist, attach some iron shackles to them, and then seal them up with mortar in the catacombs. Maybe I should wall up some of the craftsmen and vendors also.

I finally hung a set of rules on the front of my booth. 1. No food allowed. 2. No blocking the entry. 3. No littering. 4. No using my booth as a meeting place with acquaintances, even if it is raining outside. 5. No substitutions on frames and mats. 6. No touching the paintings. 7. No claiming that you or your mother could paint a piece like one of mine. 8. No trivial questions and no pontificating about art theory. 9. No negotiation on prices. 10. The main opening to my booth is 36 inches wide. If you are at least this large, no entering.

However, the manager of the show made me take the sign down.

As my sales ebbed, some of my co-workers offered tidbits of advice. One suggested, "You need a gimmick to capture the public's attention, maybe have a monkey out front, or a dwarf, or maybe a beautiful woman stretched out on a lounge chair."

Another offered, "You need to have a plant, a shill, someone who will sing your praises loudly so that passersby will hear him. Then have him 'make a purchase' to encourage others to buy from you. You could wrap up a painting you don't think will sell anyway and give it to him, or he could store it until you retrieved it at the end of the show."

Another suggested I hang signs up reminding the public that art is an investment and that mine is likely to appreciate in value. "Make up some statistics indicating that your paintings are worth three times what they sold for three years ago," he said, "and then fabricate a fake list of awards you have received. People won't know the difference, particularly if you say the awards were given in Canada."

An artist who charged particularly high prices for his own art suggested that I raise my prices. "They won't value your paintings or even consider them to be real unless they have to pay a lot for them," he said. I thanked all of them for their advice and politely demurred, though I did briefly consider hanging a sign up that said, "If you think my prices are too low, arrangements can be made for raising them."

After several months of diminishing sales, my spirits began to sag. I tried not to take the loss of sales as a rejection of me as an artist or even further as a person, but it was difficult, which in turn made my body begin to weaken, a process aided no doubt by my failure to eat much of anything. It became more difficult to set up and break down my equipment. To at least spare myself the labor of setting up a tent and risking bad weather, I began looking for more and more indoor shows, even though I had always done better outdoors. This led me to participate in two or three shows held in shopping malls, where customers were much more interested in the merchandise offered by large department stores than that offered in kiosks in the hallways.

My booth itself began to illustrate my demise. I sometimes would fail to straighten paintings that clumsy customers or the wind knocked asunder; I sometimes neglected to affix price tags and name cards, in many cases making it difficult for visitors to distinguish between originals and reprints; I often neglected to hang the sign welcoming patrons, even contemplating replacing it with a sign that simply said, "Go away"; I would overlook litter dropped on the ground in or around my booth; I gradually brought fewer and fewer paintings to the shows (rationalizing this with the belief that customers were intimidated by too many choices); and I would start packing up well before closing time (on the sly of course since the managers of the shows explicitly forbade such a practice). And as if ashamed of my own work, I often forgot to sign and date, on the backs, the few pieces I sold, and I gradually forgot to record in my ledger the amount of my sales.

To aggravate the situation even more, I was assigned locations farther and farther from the prime spots I commanded in the past. It dawned on me at one show that I was next to the pen that the humane society set up for pet adoptions on the path leading to the food vendors. This created two problems: one, I had to listen to a lot of dogs barking during the day while smelling the stench of their defecation, and, two, people rushed past my booth without even a pause so that they could feast. I realized that in the strictest sense I had become an impediment in the path to the menagerie and the food court. Plus I no longer could count on enjoying a community of artists, since very few of them still came to the shows and since I was cut off from the remaining ones by a phalanx of crafters selling dog houses, bird houses, and whirly-gigs, who hawked their wares all day long with loud voices repeating the same come-on phrases and who frequently checked on my sales as if we were all in competition.

My spirits sank so low that I was not even rejuvenated by an award for best display, which I was given at one show, a surprise to me considering my neglect. What was so disheartening was that the twenty year old singer who performed all day on the make-shift stage set up for the show was assigned to present me with the award and then kiss me on the cheek. She must have been repulsed by me, for, after draping a ribbon around my neck, from which hung a silvery pendant, and then attempting to kiss me, she broke into tears and had to be led away by the manager of the show.

Nor was I rejuvenated by an incident that took place at a show two weeks after I had skipped one which I had attended for a number of years, but during which I had seen my sales fall off by approximately sixty percent. "Hey, where were you at the Clovis Park show?" a crafter selling decorated pinecones asked.

"I decided not to do it this year," I answered.

"Well, a customer was very disappointed in you. She asked where you were—said she was thinking about buying one of your barn paintings."

"Did she say she had bought one before?"

"No, but she did mention that she had been looking at some of them for a couple of years. She thought they were really beautiful."

I halfway wished that I could have seen the woman just to explain to her exactly why I didn't set up at the show and let her know how many visitors were like her: visitors to my booth who looked but never bought any works and who thus did not understand that I had to make a living. "If you see her again, tell her I'm sorry," I said, but I didn't really mean it.

As the weeks turned into months and show led to show, I found myself withdrawing farther and farther from the public. Except for an occasional outburst of fury, during which I ordered customers out of my tent, prompting the manager of the show to offer an unctuous apology for my behavior, I simply retreated into my own heart of darkness in the back corner of my booth behind one of my display screens. My black clothes, which matched my disposition, helped hide me, particularly if I kept my melancholy face in the shadows. I simply wanted to be left alone. I did not want to talk to anyone, particularly some enthusiast who wished to take a picture of me standing in front of my art. I fell into such a funk that I did not even want to talk to children or pet someone's dog. Eating was out of the question now, not because I was sated with elation as before, but because I had no sense of a being that needed to be fed.

On the last day of a week-long show, the manager came by my booth to remind me that closing time had come some hour before. He found me in my refuge in the back corner. When he saw me, he gasped, I suppose because of my emaciation. "What can I do for you?" he asked.

"Forgive me," I whispered.

"For what?" he implored.

"I wanted everyone to admire my art."

"Everyone does, and that includes me," he responded.

"But you shouldn't admire it. I should get no credit for it. For you see..."

"Yes?"

"You see, I have to paint. It's part of my nature. My art is me. Admiring my art is the same as admiring me, but wishing for that is a sign that I am caught up in my own ego."

The manager looked up to the two or three people who had gathered in the booth to see what was happening and tapped on his forehead to signify that I had gone crazy. "Why don't we help Gregory pack up his art and display equipment. He'll be better when he gets home. Won't you, Mr. Sampson?"

.   .   .   .

I discovered a few weeks later from a visitor to my room in Ward Three that for the next show, in the spot where my display had been, there was a new food vendor that sold tangerine, lemon, and cherry sno-cones in Dixie cups that were decorated with igloos and polar bears. His booth was brightly decked out in orange, yellow, and red.

I'll bet it was hard to miss, and I bet he did a lot of business, selling to people who took their sticky fingers to other booths.

06
Hero and Leander

They met at an art gala in Sestos, which was celebrating Diana, the goddess of the moon. Leander had submitted for jurying three of his newest works, all of which had been accepted for the exhibition.

Hero was a lover of art, especially pieces having to do with the goddess Diana. She was fascinated by Leander's three works, soaking in the details as she moved from one to the other, oblivious to all the other people at the gala. One was an oil, depicting Diana surrounded by a dark background with mere hints of stars. The second one, a watercolor, centered on the moon, with almost indistinct light waves beaming down on various figures, who were reveling, embracing, drinking, somehow having a joyous occasion prompted by the presence of the moon. The third painting, an acrylic, was another portrait of Diana, smiling down on the moon, which she was holding in her hands as if were a grapefruit.

Leander himself stood a few feet away, inconspicuously leaning against a column, all the while admiring Hero's beauty. Befitting the intense heat outside (over ninety degrees at nine p.m. in February) she was dressed to look comfortable: a light blue kirtle, a simple white bodice with large loose sleeves, all made out of plain woven linen, or what was called "lawn," giving everything a silky appearance. On her head she wore a myrtle wreath, which complemented her rich, full dark brown hair and her mocha colored skin. Around her neck she wore a chain of pebble stones that glistened whenever she moved. On her feet she wore open-toed buskins, which laced up to the middle of her calves.

Slowly it dawned upon her that someone had been standing nearby the whole time she had been engrossed in the paintings. She turned to face him and was immediately taken by his appearance: hair that seemed to have never been cut, a straight, athletic body, white skin, beautiful blue eyes, cheeks that had an oriental look, full sensuous lips. Also appropriate to the weather outside, he was wearing loose cotton pants and shirt, the latter open down to where the third button normally was closed. "Are these your works?"

"Yes, I hope you like them. As the signatures indicate, my name is Leander. I'm from across the Helespont Desert in Abydon. What's your name?"

"I'm Hero, and I live here in Sestos. I've often heard of you. Aren't these night paintings a departure from your usual subject matter? Aren't you the painter famous for including some version of the sun or Apollo in every one of your works?"

"I guess so, but over a stretch of two years or so, during which the public's attitude toward the sun and its heat changed radically, I began to sell fewer and fewer of the sun pictures, reaching a point where I felt like I was under suspicion for some sort of malfeasance. Even my patron Apollo couldn't help after a while."

"I can't even remember when this horrible heat all started," Hero said. "It seems like it's always been hot in the daytime, forcing everyone to plan most activities at night, particularly the few taking place outdoors. Why did you have the sun in all your paintings?"

"Do you remember when the sun was the symbol of goodness, with song after song praising it?

"Yes, I remember.'"

"Well, that was before it got really hot and more and more people developed melanomas. More and more movies had the worst things happen in broad daylight, and of course there were fewer and fewer paintings and songs celebrating the sun. Everybody was trying to please Diana. I was simply following suit when I switched over to paintings like these three, though I think I might have made Apollo angry in the process." In the background could be heard an Elvis impersonator crooning "Blue Moon."

The whole time he was talking, Hero kept her eyes glued to his hair and face. Artist of the sun or artist of the night; it didn't matter to her. She was smitten. And so was Leander, who rattled on about the weather in order to save himself from being tongue-tied. He would have preferred to tell her how beautiful she was, but he had never been that bold before. He wanted to tell her that he wished he had seen her face before he painted the pictures of Diana so that he could have used Hero's face as the model, but he stayed on neutral subjects. "Do you remember going to the beach and soaking up the sun's rays?"

"Yes, when I a little girl, we visited a place on the coast. Each year, we had to add a little more sun block, until we were slathering on SPF 100. Then we had to stop going altogether. Now, because of the regulations, I don't dare even go out in the daytime."

Leander was thinking what a shame it was that he wouldn't get to see Hero at the beach in a bikini bathing suit. He started to comment about how many outdoor recreations had been canceled or curtailed, but he chose to pause and gaze into Hero's eyes. He moved ever so slightly toward her. At the same time, she leaned toward him. He wanted to paint a portrait of her face then and there. It certainly matched the beauty of Diana's face. She wanted to run her hands through his voluminous hair. It seemed almost godlike. At that particular moment Kim Carnes' recording of "Looking for a Big Night" was playing."

Suddenly, their moment of bliss was interrupted by a strident voice: "Hero, you should not be talking to this man!"

Hero dropped her gaze from Leander and turned to face the person that had ruined her best moment in years. "Father, why would you say such a thing? He's one of the artists at the gala."

"He's an artist all right, with a history of producing mostly paintings about the sun. He couldn't have possibly done so without being influenced by the subject matter."

Hero raised her voice. "But that's ridiculous. They're just his paintings; they aren't him."

"It's been my experience that you can't separate the art and the artist. If he paints pictures of the sun, which, as everybody knows, is an evil force, then he has the seeds of evil in him."

"Doesn't it matter that he's now painting pictures of Diana and the night? Look at these three," she said, as she swept her arm across the fronts of Leander's works.

'Those don't change anything. The damage is done. Now come with me before you become damaged by him." He grabbed her by her upper arm and half dragged her toward the exit.

Leander was stunned. He had always assumed that by painting Apollo and the sun, he was creating a force of cheerfulness. He stood staring at the three paintings on the wall. Why were they so different? In them he was glorifying Diana and darkness, a goddess and something in nature, just as in his sun paintings he had adored Apollo and the sun, a god and again something natural. He could not believe that Hero's father could be such a fundamentalist. It put him in league with those who associated dance or rock and roll music with evil and by extension with those who labeled a person as evil due to race or nationality or even religion. He scanned the room, wondering if those who had previously made the sun their main subject were now being stigmatized.

He was just beginning to circulate around the room to find out the answer, when, unexpectedly, he felt a hand on his wrist. It was Hero. "You've come back! I thought I had lost you," he gushed.

"Listen, I don't have but a minute. I told my father that I left my purse. He's waiting on me. I'm surprised he didn't come back in with me. Don't think I'm being too forward, but can you come to my house three nights from tonight on Tuesday at seven? My parents are going out to a business party. You could bring another painting or two for me to see, even ones with the sun."

"Yes, of course I'll come. I'll paint something with you in it. Where do you live?"

"On the Appian Road, 1314. It's about two miles from here. How will you get there? Do you have your own car?"

"No, we're allowed only one car per family, due to the EPA's efforts to reduce even more emissions. I had to get a special permit to drive to the Gala tonight. Somebody in the Energy Commission must be sympathetic to artists. But I'll try to get it again, but if I can't get our car, I'll figure something else out."

"Well, be safe, but please come to my place. My room is in the tower on the east end of the house." With that she turned to hurry away.

"Wait! What about your purse?"

"I guess I'll just have to say I didn't have it after all, but only thought I did." She gave a coquettish smile and was then gone.

He began early the next morning, working feverishly on a new painting, more inspired than he had ever been before. By early afternoon, he had almost completed the painting. It was a dreamy picture of Hero, a smile on her face as she looked at the moon.

Having finished most of the painting, he decided to make his case to his parents about using the family car on Tuesday, but he could not tell them his real purpose, since they, in keeping with long standing tradition, had already chosen a match for him, the only daughter of long time friends of theirs.

His best line of argument was that on Tuesday he needed to deliver the painting he was working on to a woman he had met at the gala in Sestos, a person who liked his work, all of which was true. He simply left out the part about seeing Hero without her meddling father around.

"Why didn't she buy one of the pictures you displayed at the show?" his father asked.

"I guess I slipped up and mentioned I could paint something that included her image. Here, let me show you what I came up with. I'm almost finished with it."

"She's quite pretty," his mother said after viewing his new work, "and so much detail. You must have really studied her face."

"She was easy to remember," Leander said, "but I still had to contrive a lot of it," though he knew better.

"Well, take your time finishing it," his father said. "I've got to travel to Sestos in two weeks. I can deliver it for you then."

"But . . . ."

"No buts about it. We can't use up that much of our monthly travel allotment. Plus, I'm going to need the car for the next several days to make deliveries to my customers. Don't forget that each morning you're going to help me with some of the heavier items. In the meantime I'll check around for someone who is going to Sestos. Maybe we can get it delivered that way."

After many inquiries, his father had to confess on Monday evening that he was unable to find anyone who could be helpful. Leander was of course relieved since he wanted to deliver the painting himself—and see Hero—but was dismayed in that getting to Sestos on Tuesday by car was out of the question now. He considered waiting the two weeks and riding with his father, but he knew he would not be able to hang on that long to see Hero, and he knew that it would be difficult to give the picture to her with her parents at home. He also considered hitchhiking, but the odds were that whoever stopped to give him a ride would know his parents, and he'd have some hard explaining to do if word got back that he was picked up on the highway.

After much consideration, he knew that he had only one option and that was to hike the seventeen miles to Sestos across the Helespont Desert, even though he would have to start out in the middle of the day after helping his father with deliveries. He was fit, plus, he figured Apollo would be on his side since he had painted so many pictures of the sun god or just the sun. He'd just have to cover up to block the sun and drink lots of liquids.

After helping all morning with heavy packages, Leander told his father he would be spending the rest of the day at an artists' workshop, which might even extend into the evening.

"There must be a lot of diligent artists in Abydos," his father quipped. "What goes on at a 'workshop'?"

"Oh, we try new techniques, extend ourselves a bit, and get feedback. It's very helpful."

"Try to get home early; your mother and I want to talk about your future, including your bride to be. We think she's a lovely thing."

Leander promised that he would, but as soon as his father went back to his deliveries, Leander covered his skin in sun block, dressed himself in the loosest white shirt and pants he could find, and donned extra large UV protection sunglasses, shoes sturdy enough for the long hike but light enough that he wouldn't feel as he were walking in work boots, and headgear that could have appeared in the movie *Lawrence of Arabia* on camel riders, with large overhanging flaps that covered his neck and ears. He wanted protection from the noonday sun, but did not want to look like someone in a HAZMAT outfit. He realized that he was already tired from all the lifting that morning, but the anticipation of seeing Hero lifted his spirits. After carefully wrapping up the picture of Hero, pinning a thermometer on his sleeve, and strapping several liter bottles of water around his waist, he set out, the thermometer reading 107. He figured it would take approximately six hours, maybe seven, which would put him at Hero's house about the time the parents were leaving.

The desert he was crossing had at one time been the setting for the Helespont River, but now was a barren wasteland, with scrubby bushes and a few almost dead Cyprus trees. There was not much else to look at since the sky and the desert floor were almost a continuous blur of blinding light, a yellowish-white carpet littered with rocks. Leander quickly learned to avoid stepping on the rocks since they felt as if someone had just recently used them as the base for a fire ritual or a cookout. Occasionally he would stumble and fall down after failing to spot a rock half buried in the sand, but he would gather himself and plod onward toward Sestos. After an hour, the temperature had climbed to 109, with no ameliorating wind. If Dali had stuck a clock out here, it surely would have melted and run off the table, he imagined.

As he hiked, in order to get his mind off the terrain, he thought about the causes and effects of the extreme heat. One cause was the depletion of the ozone layer, due in turn to the inexplicable reluctance of certain nations to abide by various international agreements to monitor the expulsion into the air of methane and carbon dioxide, resulting in the sun's radiation bombarded the earth's surface unrestricted, baking the earth like a broiler, causing droughts, the loss of forests, a drastic loss of crops, and a sharp increase in sun related illnesses in humans. Another reason, with equally devastating results, also created by the formation of these gasses, was the greenhouse effect, wherein heat from the earth was trapped nearer the surface, causing more intense violent weather, including hurricanes, tornadoes, flooding, and, ironically, huge snow storms, which usually melted within a day or so.

Of course there were other changes, particularly in the world of recreation. There was practically no beach crowd anymore, no spring breaks with topless contests, college students hanging out of cars with sunroofs, and places like Miami had become seedier havens of gambling, rapes, murders, and partying drunks, who slept off their nighttime excesses during the day. At the other end of the scale, winter sports simply died away.

And one could have anticipated the changes in the clothing industry, with a market mostly for lighter weaves. What one might not predict was the gradual removal of the sun as a symbol on several national flags, including Japan's, and the abandonment of long-acknowledged rituals such as sun dances and visiting sweat lodges.

As mentioned with Hero, the music and art world changed radically too. No one played "Sunshine on My Shoulder," "I'm Walking in Sunshine," "Here Comes the Sun," or any of the other countless songs that depicted the sun in a positive way. They got replaced by a revival of songs about the night or the moon: "Tonight" from *West Side Story*, Heatwave's "Boogie Nights," Neil Young's "Tonight's the Night," Louis Armstrong's "Moon River," Cat Stevens' "Moon Shadow," Tom Waits' "Drunk on the Moon," and Christmas favorites (annoyingly played year round) such as "All Through the Night," "O Holy Night," and "Silent Night, Holy Night." Pictures about the moon and the night followed suit, with Van Gogh's *Starry Night*, for instance, soaring in value. And movies about night creatures became even more popular than they had already been made by the glut of youthful looking bloodsuckers as heroes.

Leander was three hours into his journey and was feeling the effects of the 112 degrees. Even the most romantic thoughts about Hero did not keep him from picturing himself in an oven. Two or three times he pleaded, "Apollo, please turn down the heat!" He contemplated offering a sacrifice to Apollo by slaying an animal, but he had not seen one the entire journey. He was tempted to pour out one of his bottles of water onto the sand as a tribute, but he hated to give up even one. He knew there was some truth to his comment to Hero about how he had alienated Apollo by turning to Diana in his art. He came to suspect that perhaps Apollo was making it even hotter than normal just to spite him. He remembered that Apollo was known for his jealous and competitive nature. Just ask Cassandra. When she rejected Apollo's advances, Apollo made it impossible for anyone to believe her prophecies. Or ask Midas, who ended up with an ass's ears when he crossed Apollo. Leander's one consolation was that it would be nighttime when he returned, and Diana was sure to watch over him.

On he trudged, figuring he was approximately half way to Hero's. He began to wish that he could have found a way to send her picture he was carrying so that it would be waiting for him in Sestos. He found it amazing how one portrait could feel like a twenty-pound barbell. His stops for water came more and more frequent, and the water supply was dwindling. He tried to pick up his pace to get there before he had completely finished off his water, but that was like someone, low on gas, driving faster to get to the next gas station.

At around 5 pm, with Sestos only a distant, vague mirage on the horizon and the thermometer on his sleeve reading 113 degrees, he sat down for a few minutes. He was tempted to remove his clothes, hoping that his skin could feel a whisper of a breeze, but he knew better. There was no breeze, and his skin would redden and blister in practically no time.

As 7 pm arrived, he was still a good mile away with no water left, but the thought that he would soon be with Hero gave him an extra burst of energy, and although he did not move any faster, his gait no longer looked as if it were that of a wounded soldier, struggling to get back to his troops.

At last he was outside Hero's tower. It was nearly 8 pm. He had fretted over the possibility that her parents would still be at home. How would he get her attention? He needn't have worried; she was waiting in the window. "You're late," she said, not scolding him but rather conveying her concern. "My parents have been gone for an hour. I was afraid you couldn't come. How did you get here?"

"I crossed the desert on foot. I would have been here earlier except I had to help my father with some of his deliveries this morning."

"Oh, you poor dear. I can't imagine anyone out there in the heat we've had today. You must be exhausted."

"I'm all right," he asserted with more bravado than he actually felt.

"Let's not waste any more time. Go through the door to your right and come to the top of the stairs. I'll be waiting for you."

With the temperature still above 100 degrees, all Leander could think about was cooling off. "Can I take a shower somewhere?"

"The only place for that is in my room, but . . ."

"What's wrong?" he asked.

"I suppose it will be all right."

"I promise to behave," he said, with a slight smile.

Upon reaching her room, he unwrapped the painting and presented it to her. "Oh, it's so lovely. How in the world did you produce it so quickly?"

"I was inspired. Your face could launch a thousand paintings."

"You're so kind. And to think you carried it all the way across the desert. Now if you want that shower, it's through this door," she said as she gestured to her right. "Meanwhile, I'm going to study your painting."

Leander enjoyed the shower more than any he had ever taken, but cut it short so that he could be with Hero. After toweling off, he realized that he would have to put back on the dirty and sweaty clothes he had worn through the desert. Maybe Hero had something he could wear—at least a robe. He called out to her, but got no answer. He tried again, with the same results.

Finally, holding the towel around his waist, he stepped out into the bedroom. Hero was at the window, holding the new picture as is she wanted to see it in the early moonlight. He spoke her name again, but she was so mesmerized by the picture she still didn't hear him. At last, he walked to her and touched her shoulder. She jerked in surprise, almost dropping the painting, and, more importantly, causing Leander to lose his grip on the towel. Suddenly Hero found herself in a situation she had never been in before: standing face to face with a naked man.

Her reaction was to let out a mild scream and then, inexplicably, run to her bed, where she buried herself under her covers. Leander wrapped the towel back around his waist and followed her to the bed, where he sat down.

"How could you!" she exclaimed in a muffled tone from under the covers. "Did you think I'd just jump in your arms because you've got no clothes on?"

"Please, Hero. I didn't want to put back on my dirty clothes. I should have brought extras, but they would have been just that much more weight to carry in the desert. I hollered to you to see if you had anything I could wear, but you didn't answer. I'm terribly sorry the towel slipped. I didn't mean anything by it. Please come out and talk to me. I'm covered up now."

Slowly Hero peeled back the covers of her bed and emerged. "You certainly startled me. I'm sorry I reacted so dramatically. I've never had a man in my room. I once swore an oath to the goddess Venus to preserve my chastity until after I marry, so I have always avoided the temptation of opening my door to a man, except my father of course, who checks on me routinely."

"I can imagine that there are hundreds of men in just Sestos alone who would love to be where I am at this moment. You're the most beautiful woman I've ever seen. That's why it was so easy to paint your picture. I imagined I was painting Diana."

Hero was not immune to the power of Leander's words, particularly since she had fallen in love with him at first sight. She listened, blushed, and listened some more as Leander flattered, cajoled, whispered sweet nothings, persuaded, slowly making her discover what her heart was already telling her.

"I love what you are saying and would gladly invite you to lie with me in bed, but I did make the vow to Venus."

"But isn't Venus the goddess of love? Isn't swearing allegiance to her a major step in enjoying passion and fulfillment? Wouldn't she want you to enjoy the night with me? Treasures are neglected when misers keep them, and there is little difference in the appearance of the finest gold and the basest metal when allowed to go unused. If you build a castle and keep the gate closed, it becomes ruinous and desolate. Beauty is lost if kept too warily. Besides, what is virginity? It is not of the earth or heaven, but is a mere thought. Things that do not exist are never lost. If you want to become a true follower of Venus, then reconsider your notion of chastity. True chastity, as Venus would have it, is enjoying the love and passion we have between us."

Leander plied Hero with these and other not-so-subtle persuasions, which, though probably corny to most people, struck deep within the heart of Hero.

Of course Hero pretended to resist his arguments, even faking anger at various points, but she was already won. Eventually, she pulled back the covers and waited as he slid between the sheets. It was the beginning of a seizing of rapture, interrupted only once when her parents came home, giving the pair of lovers more than ample warning as they drove into the driveway, closed the front door, and noisily climbed the steps to Hero's tower. Hero had gathered Leander's dirty clothes and the new painting and put them under her bed, shortly before ushering him under there too.

"How was the party?" she asked from her bed, as she held up a book as if she had been reading.

"Like most business parties we've gone to," her father answered. "I hope your evening was more exciting than ours, even if it was just reading a book."

"Were you bored?" her mother asked.

"Far from it," Hero said with almost too much enthusiasm. "You know how much I get into something that I love."

Assuming that Hero was referring to the book, her mother pulled at her husband. "I'm tired. Let's allow her to get back to her reading. See you in the morning, dear." With that they closed her door and were gone.

After waiting until the lights went off in her parents' bedroom, Hero invited Leander from under the bed to join her in bed again. Their love making was even more passionate than before, except they were more careful about crying out in their highest moments of ecstasy. He asked nothing and she denied nothing.

At about two in the morning, Hero pushed back from Leander and said, "Shouldn't you be on your way about now if you're going to cross the desert in the nighttime?"

"Yes, I should, and I will soon, but come back into my arms for just a last few minutes."

Holding each other in a loving embrace, they talked in tender tones about their love, their love making, the picture he had brought to her, and future plans for meeting again. Each moment made them more comfortable with the other—and more relaxed. Soon both of them had drifted into a pleasant slumber.

The next thing they heard was Hero's father calling up the steps to her tower. "Hero, it's almost eight. Remember that you have an appointment at the dentist's at nine. Do I need to come up to help?"

Hero, suddenly fully awake, answered her father, "Oh, no, I can manage. I'll be right down." She then extricated herself from Leander's loving embrace and leapt from the bed. "Leander, you've got to leave quickly. My father might decide to come on up here any minute. Here, take your clothes and dress quickly. You can go out the back way."

Leander dressed as fast as he could, but putting on his clothes from the day before reminded him of the formidable task lying ahead. Hero understood this also and asked, "How can you possibly cross the desert two days in a row in the sun?"

"I'll manage somehow. I have our night together to reflect upon. That thought will sustain me. Besides, I'm still starting almost four hours earlier that I did yesterday."

After filling his water bottles and giving Hero a passionate kiss, he left, fortunately avoiding meeting with her parents on the way out.

It did not take him long to discover that the difference between the heat at 8 am and that at noon was not great. It was already 99, and Leander could feel fatigue in his whole body, a product of helping his father the day before, the previous day's hike through the desert, and the night with the lovely Hero. At least he was not carrying the painting he had brought for Hero.

By noon, with the thermometer reading 105, he was as exhausted as he had been the previous day at the end of the journey. The air was so thick he felt as if he were swimming in hot water. Every step was a labor.

Two hours later, his progress toward Abydos slowing by the mile, his water supply now dwindled down to one bottle, and the temperature at 112, he knew he was in trouble. His only salvation was to keep moving.

As he continued on, he began to worry if he had done the wrong thing with Hero. Should he feel guilty for his persuasive words? Was he totally responsible for her giving in? Was Venus out to get him for twisting her role and ideas to suit his own desires? Was Apollo punishing him for painting yet another picture glorifying Diana? Apollo, he rationalized, was not just the god of the sun, but also the god of medicine and healing. Surely, he would not let Leander perish in the desert. Venus, he wasn't so sure about.

The fretting only succeeded in sapping much of his remaining energy, so he collected himself and pressed on, drinking sparingly from his last bottle. It seemed as if it was taking longer to cross the desert this time, and, in fact, it was. It was already four in the afternoon, the thermometer reading a blistering 114. He tried crying out for help, hoping someone in the outskirts of Abydos would hear him, but his throat was so dry, the only sound that came out of him was a low-pitched gasp, even after he drank the remaining water from his last bottle.

He knew he could not go on under the existing circumstances. He needed desperately to rest. "What if I lie down in the sand and wait until evening, when it won't be as hot?" he thought. That would surely work, he believed. And while he rested, he would call upon Diana, who he figured owed him one for doing all those paintings of her, to bring on the night more quickly.

He found a loose rock to turn over, figuring that, despite the heat of the rock's top, the sand beneath it would be cooler, but he could hardly move it. After much wrestling and struggling, he cleared a place in the sand to lie down. It did not take long for him to imagine that he was back with Hero, lying with her on her sheets. Like the sand, she was naked. Slowly he removed his own clothes so he could press himself to her. She offered no resistance. They fell asleep together as they had the night before, except there was no waking up.

Somewhere, Diana sighed for the loss of another good artist, one who made her look beautful in every painting. But she knew that the seed of a new artist was growing in Sestos.

07
Placid

Arnel Lightwing, landscape artist, sat at his easel, knowing that he was in the right place.

He lived on an island called Placid, located in the Pacific Ocean on the same latitude as the south island of New Zealand. It was endowed with scenes that he loved to capture in his paintings, including snow-capped ranges running down it from north to south, clear flowing mountain streams and waterfalls, and, oxymoronically, Hawaiian-like beaches. These beaches were bordered by lush tropical growth, which included pineapple trees, sugar cane, and papayas, on which much of the economy depended.

At the present moment, he was set up in the island's hundred acre arboretum, located halfway up the mountain between the beaches and the mountain tops, painting a watercolor of a red maple. In the past he had painted many pictures of the trees here that were noted for their fall colors—aspens, poplars, beeches, sassafras—but he also had depicted others growing in the park: nut bearing trees, including walnuts and hickories, fruit bearing trees, including cherries, apples, limes, and peaches, and a wide variety of evergreens, including firs, balsams, pines, hemlocks, and cedars.

He had been commissioned to paint this picture, as was often the case, by his patron, the ruling king named Prospero, who bought many of Arnel's pieces as well as those by other island artists, even though he himself was an artist that also painted scenes of natural beauty. He filled his palace with these works.

"Work some of your magic," Prospero requested.

"I'll try," Arnel responded, "but you're the true magician. There's an aura surrounding all your works."

A shared belief in artistic magic was not all they had in common. Though Prospero was about twenty years older than Arnel, they resembled each other physically. Both were tall, handsome, clean-shaven, with squared off jaws, Roman noses, wavy hair that was never too short nor too long, and bodies that signified time spent in the gym or on the many hiking and running trails on the island. They both liked sleek cars, Prospero having a taste for Jaguar XKEs and Lamborghinis, Arnel for restored Datsun 240Zs. Prospero, speaking for both of them, declared, "I like a vehicle that appears to slide through the wind." They also both enjoyed fine dining with vegetarian cuisine, and each loved music, especially classical symphonies. They also shared a preference for "artistic" sports that required a high degree of gracefulness and/or adherence to well defined rules of order, such as golf, tennis, or chess. They both abhorred any sports that victimized animals, particularly hunting, even rodeos.

Most importantly, though, was their shared love of beautiful scenes, though they did playfully argue about which type of painting from the past was the most compelling. "I opt for the works by the Impressionists, Monet, Renoir, Manet, and the like," said Prospero. "I love their dream-like vagueness."

"I prefer the dream-like quality that is present in the grand landscapes of Joshua Reynolds and Thomas Cole," Arnel replied. Neither made a case for artists that purposefully painted scenes of ugliness and depravity.

by Joseph Meigs

They also believed that as much of the island's natural beauty should be preserved, at the expense of economic growth. Neither wanted developers to ruin the coastlines with condominiums and hotels.

Prospero trusted Arnel completely, such that he sent the young artist on long missions around the world to discover what other people were doing to create beauty. "Go look at planned gardens, even those located at those irritating places called theme parks," he said.

Arnel's first response was, "We live in an Eden already. If Emily Dickinson was correct in saying that nature is its own church, then this island has to be the granddaddy of all cathedrals."

Prospero said in return, "We both believe in the paradoxical humanistic idea, fostered in the Renaissance period, which holds that nature is perfect as is, but humans can still improve upon it. Let's see what we can do."

When Arnel returned from his beauty-seeking explorations, he and Prospero set out to enlarge upon their Eden. First, Prospero hired the best horticulturist he could find, who worked with Prospero and Arnel to supplement the flora around the state house grounds, adding flowering shrubs and bushes, as well as artistically arranged patches of flowers that were designed so that something was always in bloom year round. Then they all joined together to plan scenic running and hiking trails throughout the island.

"You were right," Arnel said. "We can improve upon nature. It's another form of magic."

Everything seemed to be nearly perfect for Arnel and Prospero, but one day, when Arnel was delivering to Prospero a painting of a waterfall, he found his king in a sullen mood. "What's up?" he asked.

"I've got troubles. My brother, Antonio, who left the island before you came here, has decided to return."

"You've not talked about him before. Where's he been?"

"In America, making lots of money, probably through insider trading."

"Why does it bother you that he's coming back?"

"I'm afraid he might not be alone. My informants tell me that he wants to take over the throne. He believes he could do more for the economy than I can, which really means he thinks he can improve his own financial well being. Before he went away, he was an outspoken critic of my so-called liberalism, my taste for art, and my love of nature. That ingrate! And to think, I once saved his ass when his ship capsized off our coast in a storm."

"Is there anyway I can help?"

"I don't know if anybody can help me if he really wants to usurp my power. I won't offer much resistance. I think warfare is the ugliest endeavor mankind can undertake, the ultimate grotesqueness, with man killing man, leaving behind torn and rotting bodies and bombed and broken buildings."

Within a week Antonio swept into power in a bloodless coup, backed by a large contingency of soldiers that had once supported Prospero, but were persuaded by Antonio's bombast about more prosperous times ahead. True to his words to Arnel, Prospero offered no resistance, abdicating his throne and heading into exile in the neighboring country of Rockport, which had its own history of loving art. Just before he left, he told Arnel, "Tell the other artists that I'm sorry to have to desert them. I guess all of you will have to fend for yourselves. Knowing Antonio, I suspect that you'll be exposed to a whole new concept of art."

It did not take long for Antonio to impose his taste on everyone. In keeping with his claims of improving the economy, he began selling timber, cutting down native and imported trees and sending them to whichever country was willing to pay the most for them. He favored clear-cutting over selective cutting, claiming that the barren ground was a sign of economic progress, though he probably would have cut trees down just to simplify things. In several instances, the spaces left by his harvesting were used to raise cattle, which he saw as a bonus.

by Joseph Meigs

He also revamped the tourist industry, commissioning the construction of many tall hotels along the beaches, ones with large swimming pools that he deemed to be far better locations for swimming than the sea. The deforestation that made room for these buildings did not bother him in the least.

His disregard for the natural flora was matched by his attitude toward the fauna, which, he announced, "was fair game for hunters," a group of which he was an active member. In fact, he ordered that one large room of the statehouse be reserved for his diverse gun collection. "Hunting," he declared, "is a real man's sport, along with hockey, rugby, boxing, and American football, you know, ones that allow a guy to exert his power."

This approach to sports was mirrored by his choice of vehicles and food. He drove rugged and utilitarian vehicles, ones that mostly looked like large boxes: Hummers, Cadillac Escalades, vans that looked as if they were an obese person squatting on the highway, and pick up trucks with camper tops. Any car that had graceful lines he tabbed as "sissy rides."

His taste in food ran to the everyday fare also; he was a beef eater, much to the detriment of the cow population, serving it at all state dinners without ever offering a vegetarian alternative to his guests. "If they show up in my place, they'll eat what I give'em," he was fond of saying. His snacks often consisted of food that had a high sugar, salt, or fat content, his favorites being hot dogs and deep fried pork skins.

One day he summoned all the artists, including Arnel. He told them, "I'm planning to replace the art left behind by my predecessor. I want to put in some 'everyman's art' and get rid of this silliness with trees and waterfalls. Hell, if I want to look at that stuff, I can go out on the island and see plenty."

Then he turned their attention to his collection of ceramic animals placed haphazardly around the state room: elephants, flamingoes, horses, and, ironically, cows. Singling out Arnel, he said, "I understand you were one of Prospero's favorite artists. Tell me what you think of my zoo in this room."

Arnel hesitated, unsure how to answer. Finally, he said, "It's great, sir, better than the one William Randolph Hearst kept. Maybe even better since you don't have to feed them."

Seemingly oblivious to Arnel's sarcasm, Antonio continued, "And how about my new paintings?" He waved his hand around to indicate pictures depicting war and brutal sexuality. "I bet you've not done many like them."

"You're right, I haven't, but I think they fit you perfectly." Again, Antonio seemingly missed the irony in Arnel's comment.

In the weeks that followed, Arnel began to notice the effect Antonio created by his own brand of the anti-aesthetic. Instead of commenting on the metaphorical elephant in the state room or the emperor's new clothes, citizens began collecting the same kind of fake art that Antonio–the anti-artist–favored, purchased at big box stores, the kind that Propero had disdained. They began wearing the same type of clothes their new king wore in public: tight-fitting, tacky t-shirts with short sleeves rolled up above the armpits, plaid shorts that clashed with their t-shirts, untied basketball shoes, and garish, multicolored socks. They also began sporting a crop of discordant tattoos and added an excess of jewelry, which hung from their ears, eyelids, noses, lips, and perhaps other more private parts of their bodies. Strident, heavy metal music became the norm.

Arnel abhorred these developments and did his best to continue with renditions of beauty that Prosper would have approved of. Antonio was his most scathing critic, saying, "If you're going to paint, then paint pieces that people actually want to look at, something true and real, not this dreamy and unreal world you've created. When you do, I might consider buying one, if you give me the right deal." Undeterred, Arnel pressed on with his portrayals of beauty, selling to members of the public that still shared his sense of aesthetics.

But as Antonio gained sway over the minds of the public and ugliness became the new norm, Arnel found that he was selling fewer and fewer of his works—the same works that would have sold immediately upon completion in the past—leaving him struggling to make ends meet. He felt as if he was becoming an outcast, like a practitioner of a religion that a great part of the populace despised. Eventually becoming desperate, he began to rationalize: "I've included tiny flaws in my depictions of beauty before without being criticized, so I should be able to include other blemishes without losing the integrity of my art."

Thus, he began to paint in flaws, not necessarily to augment the beauty of the subject, but as ends in themselves, such as a scar with stitch marks on the face of a handsome man, arthritic fingers on the hands of an otherwise beautiful woman, pimples, crooked noses, sinister lips, badly done tattoos, and the like. His sales improved, but only slightly, still with none to Antonio.

So he increased what he now called "the ugliness factor": a factory smokestack spewing effluvium in the far background of a landscape depicting rhododendrons; an overflowing trash can at the bottom of a painting of a beautiful girl making an apple pie; overly large, beefy hands on an otherwise delicate looking woman in her garden tending a hibiscus bush.

Another step up (or down) the scale of ugliness entailed purposefully distorting certain objects in his paintings, creating an even stronger degree of visual cacophony, such as a boat that sat on top of the water rather than partially in the water; mountain ranges that progressively got more distinct the farther back they sat; distant trees that were larger than similar trees in the foreground; barns that were tilted at the wrong angles, cocked in a way that made the viewer dizzy; and cows and horses with unequal length legs. His sales did pick up, but the buyers were ordinary citizens without the means Prospero had offered, still with no interest from Antonio.

While still feeling guilty about his own metamorphosis, he went all out to please the king. He first studied the paintings of

Hieronymus Bosch, the photographs of Richard Avedon, and then ugly villains in films—including the vampire in *Nosferatu*, Freddy Krueger from *Nightmare on Elm Street*, the salivating creature in *Alien*, Todd Browning's "Freaks," the protagonist in *Hellraisers*, who patches himself back together by stealing parts from others, the wicked witch from The *Wizard of Oz*, and Mr. Creosote from *Monty Python's The Meaning of Life*. He then produced several portraits with these characters, working in clashing colors, skewed spacing, and a total disregard for tonality. None of it qualified as the grotesque, it being an art form all in itself, but rather it was simply bad art, an exercise in ugliness. He hung these in a gallery and then invited Antonio to drop by and see them. After viewing them, Antonio said to Arnel, "These are more like it. I want several of them for my personal collection."

Under Antonio's patronage, it did not take long before Arnel held as important a place—as the King's artist—as he had under Prospero. Frequently, Antonio would contact him, requesting a specific painting, such as one depicting a raucous crowd of drunks in a teeming bar next to a swimming pool filled with bloated swimmers, telling Arnel to spare no expense. He even paid for Arnel to fly to the United States to attend the World's Ugliest Dog Contest, where he sketched a detailed drawing of the winner, as well as several others, all of which he converted to oil paintings when he returned to Placid. Arnel was elated by his success, though he still felt guilty because there was no magic in the paintings.

Arnel was resigned to his new role, but then another alteration in the political landscape arose. For whatever reason, Antonio's popularity began to wane. Maybe it was because he overtaxed the fruit and sugar industries and the condominium owners; maybe it was the way he kept adding square footage to the statehouse, which he preferred to call his "citadel," or maybe people simply got tired of his taste in art, sculpture, music, clothes, and more. Whatever the reason, his own army turned against him and called for Prospero to return. Antonio became an exile much as Prospero had been, only he had a much more difficult time finding a country that would grant him asylum, his reputation for ugliness having preceded him. Whereas Antonio had ridden into the city, during his usurpation, in a boxy military Jeep, wearing a loose fitting, olive drab uniform, Prospero came back in a sleek Ferrari, wearing a handmade suit that fit him perfectly.

Prospero's first action upon returning to power was to call in the artists that had previously painted beautiful scenes, Arnel being the first. "What have you done in my absence?" he asked.

Arnel was momentarily stumped about how to respond. Did he admit to producing ugly works simply to survive as an artist but was in no way persuaded to like what he was doing? He knew Prospero would say, "So you sold out and went against your basic nature, right?"

Should he claim that he had been led astray by Antonio during Prospero's absence, like a backsliding sinner, while being able to overlook Antonio's clothing, food, and economic policies, and was now ready to return to the fold, even more zealous to paint beauty? Should he make an attempt to justify Antonio's penchant for the ugly, persuading Prospero that beauty abounds even in the ugly? Should he admit to Prospero (after having already done so with himself) that he rather enjoyed painting pictures of the ugly?

Instead of answering these nagging questions directly, he decided to show Prospero what he had done. He of course started with the work he produced soon after Prospero was ousted, paintings that still displayed beauty. "These are great," Prospero effused, "but why are they not sold?"

"They didn't appeal to Antonio or the public that followed his lead," Arnel answered in a meek voice.

"Well, then, show me something else," Prospero ordered. Arnel reluctantly revealed the paintings in which he had experimented with flaws, hoping Prospero would not notice.

He did, but he was tactful in his response. "I like them, but tell me why you included that scar on the side of the subject's face."

"As you remember, sir, I've included flaws in some of my earlier portraits, a mole here, a birthmark there, on a beautiful woman. I treated the scar as a masculine counterpart to the moles and marks on a woman."

"I see," Prospero answered, "but you may have gone just a bit too far. Show me some more."

Arnel displayed others for him, paintings that he had done with greater flaws in them, works that were too artistic for Antonio, but ones he knew, judging by the grimaces and sighs, were disturbing to Prospero. "That's about it," Arnel said. "Antonio bought the rest of them." He knew he would be in trouble if Prospero went searching for them in the statehouse.

He did, mainly because Antonio, in his haste to leave the country, had left them hanging–in a separate gallery from all the rest of his acquisitions, but nonetheless in plain view. Upon discovering them, Prospero called for Arnel. This time he was not so tactful. "Have you lost your mind?" he shouted.

Arnel did not waste time trying to explain why he had painting such ugliness, though he knew in his heart that he had come to like these productions, even more than those with scenic beauty. He said, "Remember how we once talked about the classical notion that 'art improves upon nature,' and that even ugliness could be transformed into beauty in the hands of an artist?"

"Yes, I know all that," Prospero responded in a gruff voice. "But this isn't an improvement upon nature; it's simply a copying of the worst of nature."

Arnel knew that Prospero was right, but his own desire was to paint more of the same. At the same time, he did not want to lose Prospero's patronage. "I will paint you some pieces that will please you. Just give me a couple of weeks."

And he did, only he was constantly nagged by more guilt–guilt arising from the feeling he was not being true to himself, that he was selling out in the same way he had when first painting for Antonio. His finished products were beautiful, and Prospero liked them, but Arnel found himself in his spare time going back to depictions of the ugly—city landfills, milk cartons, rats, and the like. He kept them hidden of course, but he often pulled them out and admired them while he was alone. He began to form his own theory of art—that in order to be true, art must include the unseemly, the unattractive, the repulsive. He remembered watching the movie *Barton Fink*, the message of which was that in order to be good at his profession, a writer must take a spin through hell. Maybe Antonio's world was a kind of hell, but a necessary stop on the artistic journey.

He continued to paint for Prospero, giving the king the kind of art that won Arnel a lucrative patronage. But for himself he continued painting the ugly, the less acceptable form of beauty to some, but another form of true beauty to his way of thinking.

In time, he found pleasure in all of his paintings, both those for Prospero and those for himself. He came to appreciate more and more the notion of the "democratic aesthetic," espoused by Walt Whitman, who, as expressed in "Song of Myself," believed there was beauty in everything, whether it be "ripples," "the shine and shade on the trees," "mountains misty-topt," or "blacksmiths with grimed and hairy chests" or even that which is removed by a surgeon and "drops horribly in a pail."

What would he do if Prospero discovered his personal collection of the ugly? What would he do if Antonio rose to power again and found that Arnel had returned to painting for Prospero? He figured he would cross those bridges when the time came. The good thing was that he had broadened his conception of what he considered beautiful and come to realize that there is much truth in the notion that beauty is in the eye of the beholder. He realized that an artist did not necessarily need an island like Placid to create inspiring art, that there could be magic everywhere if the artist felt it.

He definitely felt the magic.

08
Art Stroll

"Ronald, I've got a big favor to ask."

"Ask away," I responded, but with lots of reservations. It's always been hard to read Gertrude Ginzer when she approaches you for anything, particularly "favors." She could be asking for a small donation to the Public School Art Fund, or she might just as likely be asking for you to remove a locomotive that ran aground in her front yard. This time it was something in between.

"As you know, we at the County Arts Council, in cooperation with the town, are going to restart the first Friday evening art strolls after a nearly two year's hiatus. I've been asked to be the curator for the County Art Gallery again, but as you know, I did it for five years, and plus, I have an ailing husband, who needs me almost full time now. The members of the Arts Council agreed that if I can't do it, then you're the right person for it. You almost always displayed some of your works when we did have the strolls and attended most of the openings. Plus you get along well with the people in town. You'd be perfect for the job."

My first reaction was to run away and pretend I didn't hear her, but I got to thinking that the title of curator (or some comparable title,

by Joseph Meigs

such as gallery director) might look good on my business card.

"It's not like you have to be at the gallery all the time. The stroll occurs only once a month, and I must emphasize that it is a 'stroll,' with all the associated imagery of moving at a leisurely pace. It should be no trouble at all for someone with your skills. It's our most important event each month, helping to bring in more visitors on that one night than we'll see the rest of the month. All the surrounding towns are planning to do a stroll this year."

I wanted to say that if all the nearby towns were putting on a stroll, maybe we didn't need to, since there were limited numbers of real art aficionados in the area collectively, but she was right about how the stroll night was by far our busiest time of the month. "Do you have any guide I could use for setting up?" I asked.

"Good heavens, no," she exclaimed. "Nothing ever goes as planned. I always used my instincts, you know, played it by ear. You can do that in a pinch."

This did not bode well. "It all sounds a bit half baked to me," I said.

"Oh, no, it's fully baked, at least it will be when you get some minor things done. Keep in mind that there are able members and artists who are willing to help, and, once again, I think you're the best person for the job. You can really help out the art community."

Despite Gertrude's notoriety for devious persuasion, I actually believed that she was sincere on this issue, so, with some doubt, I consented, hoping I was not making a big mistake. It's amazing how acquiring a power title can sway our choices.

"When is the first stroll?"

"Well, today is March tenth. You've got four weeks to get ready for the April fifth show. You'll have to get hustling on the advertising, and, oh, you'll have to come up with a theme for each show so that the artists know what paintings and photographs to bring, and of course you'll have to make plans for serving snacks and wine, but you can do all of that easily. So, I'll leave the stroll in your capable hands." She flashed a slightly crooked smile and then scurried away.

It's now November 11, and we've just finished our seventh and last stroll for the year. I'm trying to put together a report about it all, though it will be difficult staying positive. As I might have expected, problems abounded, some seemingly even bigger than removing a locomotive from a yard.

It started with the supposedly simple task of choosing a theme for each show. There were lots of suggestions—usually motivated by what an artist had in stock. Bob Dangerfold offered this: "I'd like to see us use the color green as a theme. It calls to mind nature."

Mary Laughter suggested, "I like having a color as our theme, but maybe yellow, making everything bright and cheerful."

Two others pushed for holiday related colors, red, white and blue in the July show, orange and black in October. Robbie Nightfellow wanted a series of seascapes, even though the gallery was located in the mountains. Gail Twirlly opted for a month of nudes— preferably self-portraits. The most sullen member requested that we devote one month to existential bleakness and related themes such as loneliness and alienation. A religious fanatic in the group, who always wore a white robe and called himself Jesus, insisted that we go with "all God's creatures."

We ended up going with the very generic names of "spring unfolding," "early summer," "summer's heat," "early fall," "fall in all its splendor," "the coming of winter," and "winter's bleakness," and of course received a chorus of objections (including, "I never paint any works about the summer or the fall"). Somehow, with a stretching of the imagination, we managed to put up a show for each theme.

But it didn't come easily, even though I was joined by two quite reliable and diligent artists, Fran Maker and John Graham.

Setting up the shows was the biggest headache. First, there were structural problems, not just in the actual art, but in the structures of the frames and matting. Frequently, an artist would bring in a damaged painting—one with broken glass, another with collapsed, uneven matting, many of them with mildew, mold, or dirt spots showing inside the glass. Some pieces came with no hanging wire attached to the back (sometimes replaced by fraying string), while others came with the detested center round hook or the saw blade bar (neither of which could ever be set right so the painting hung evenly). All of this was done despite the fact that we sent out notices on what to include for hanging a work. Some artists seemed to have gathered up their remainders–perhaps some of their worst art–and submitted it, perhaps because they had their best works already hanging somewhere else.

More annoying than the structural difficulties were ones involving egos, which in some cases grew out of the structural problems. For example, when Bob Dordus discovered that we had rejected his unframed painting, he complained loudly that we had already hung another artist's work, with no frame around it. Though I wanted to tell him we rejected his because it was a crappy painting, I said, with as much tact as I could muster, "You're right, but if you'll notice, the one already hanging has a wrap around canvas, where the sides are continuations of the front."

Another artist, Clive Flannigan, moaned, "Mine's practically in the dark."

Joan Luffley declared, "Mine's too far out of the main flow of the exhibition, so nobody is even going to see it."

Molly Johnson whined, "You've put mine right between two paintings that are more vivid than mine. It's almost lost on the wall."

One particularly surly participant resigned from the Art Council because her piece was hung in a room she "didn't feel comfortable in." I caught Molly Fingerhead taking down a piece we had already hung and was in the act of replacing it with one of her own when I stopped her. I wondered what she was planning to do with the piece she removed–hide it in a storage bin? I could imagine finding it months later while searching for paper plates.

Complicating matters further, we often had to figure in the placement of the works of a "featured artist," who was allowed to hang twice as many as the usual three for any one artist, which, as one might expect, caused a new round of problems with egos. Joan Luffley added to her earlier complaint, "Why does he get more space than I do? I'm a member, too."

The artists' egos continued to manifest themselves on the night of the opening as they tried desperately to steer patrons to their own works, bedazzling them with pedantic commentary about the use of light, chiaroscuro, modality, and other topics of wonder, disregarding one of the basic principles of the organization of furthering an appreciation for the arts and for each of the participating members.

And it wasn't just the egos of contributing artists we had to deal with. On several occasions other members of the Art Council popped in, wanting to "do their part" in helping with the show. I suggested to Freddy Klingman, "Why don't you bring some pot luck item for our food table," but he insisted, "No, I want to hang the pieces."

He joined a growing group of generals, who each had his own ideas on how to conduct the war. One of these generals was Virginia Clummer, who was punctilious and precise and demanded that we use a tape measure, a t-square, a spacing bar, and, if I heard it correctly, a slide rule. "The only trouble with doing that," I told her, "is that the walls and floors are all askew from years of the building's settling, and no amount of measuring will even things out."

She finally left in a huff, claiming, "You just don't understand my obviously superior sense of proportion and balance."

Diametrically opposed to Freddy and Virginia were helpers who claimed some kind of intuition when it came to arranging pictures (and probably flowers, too). What resulted from their "arrangements" was a mishmash of shapes that could have been a visual counterpart to Jonathan

Swift's cacophony when the musicians of Lilliputia together played what they each believed was the music of the spheres. Fran Maker. John Graham and I had to start over each time this happened.

Complementing the structural and ego problems were ones having to do with timing and coordination. We set the absolute deadline for submissions on Monday at noon before the Friday stroll to give ourselves ample time to arrange the entries by colors, sizes, subject matter, verticality or horizontalness, continuity, spacing between, etc. In any case it threw a large sized tube of gesso into the operation when someone was late bringing in a piece, especially so if it was Friday afternoon just before the show was to open and we were already in a flurry of last minute activity. Hugh Cluffman did this, saying, "Just stick it anywhere," but he was miffed later when he discovered that we had hung it in the only remaining place: in semi-darkness at the end to the back hall. He also was offended when he read the newspaper article that came out two days earlier, which did not mention his name as a participant in the show. "You should have known that I'd bring something in," he cried.

Abusing deadlines took another form in regard to advertising. Our publicity representative, Bob Mechanel, knew that information about the next stroll needed to be submitted to the newspapers by Friday a week before the stroll, so that the information could be published on the next Wednesday. Did he get the notifications in on time?

Not once.

I spent much of my Mondays pleading with the editor of the newspaper: "I know we're late, but please accept this write-up about the stroll. We need all the publicity we can get."

Each time, she would glare at me for several seconds (as if I were the one responsible for the tardiness) and then say, "Okay, just this once."

Several times I found myself promising her that sometime in the next year we would take out larger ads in her paper for the gallery, budget permitting (which it never did).

Though the last hour or so before the show should have been a period of winding down, it was far from it. Fran covered the tasks of vacuuming and setting up an easel out front with a poster affixed announcing the night's show. Bob was responsible for turning on some music, making sure the guest sign-in book was in its proper place with a functioning pen, and making a quick run up and down the street to remind merchants to stay open later than normal to give visitors a greater variety of shopping possibilities. I was responsible for setting out table clothes, name tags, cups, plates, forks, toothpicks, the punch bowl (requiring ice), and, of course, the food consisting of a either a meat and cheese tray or a fruit tray, flanked by cheese balls, salsa, and crackers that members brought, and a red and a white wine (careful to keep the label of the more expensive wine showing, while pouring the cheaper wine into a carafe and discarding the bottle).

Together, we also had to arrange the chairs so that small groups could sit together and discuss the paintings, but not have the chairs blocking the flow of movement.

No matter how carefully we set up the food and drink table, there were always mishaps as the evening wore on, starting with lots of spilt punch and wine on the white table clothes or the carpet. These faux pas seemed minor, however, when compared to those created by visitors from whom you would expect better manners—artistically inclined people —who ignored the toothpicks, forks, and plates and used their fingers to harvest food from the table, food which they kept in the palm of their hand. One night I spotted a fly that kept landing on the food, but after all the marauding fingers in the food, I simply ignored it (and made sure I didn't eat any of the food it had touched).

How long visitors stayed was also a bother. There were some who seemed to have nothing to do for the evening except to sit and pontificate about their theories of art. They usually stayed long enough to whittle away much of the food stock. At the other extreme (and much more plentiful) were the visitors who seemed to be on a self timer and stayed no more than a few seconds in any given room. Maybe they thought that constant movement would make them immune to any artist trying to sell a painting.

The most troublesome visitors were those who made an appearance within five minutes of closing time, usually assuring us, "We'll be here for just a minute." Twenty or thirty minutes later, as they were finally leaving, they would say, "Sorry we took so long. It was all too beautiful." Of course, they never bought any pieces. I would have asked Gertrude Ginzer how she got the loiterers out, but she never came to any of the strolls.

As one might guess (and as Gertrude certainly knew), there was a huge gulf between the optimism leading up to the shows and the harsh and disillusioning reality that came with the shows. There were only a few sales spread out over the various art strolls, probably reduced because we refused to bargain, a practice necessitated by the fact that the artist sets the price and we have to abide by his wishes. But none of us would have bargained anyway. It seemed beneath us.

For the most part, people treated the gallery as if it were a museum, full of interesting pieces that could never be bought. We could sympathize with a hostess that spent days fixing an elaborate and artistic meal, only to have no one show up, or if they did, merely criticize the layout and eat nothing.

The art strolls made me understand that the hardest part of being an artist is not always the creative process of putting paint to paper or onto a canvas. An art stroll may be a "stroll" for people out for a leisurely evening, during which they drop into a gallery, eat some food there, glance around, and then move on, but for a curator it is a marathon run in inclement weather.

Each show did have something positive. Fran, John and I had the pleasure of judging and appreciating new art each month. No critters (mice, bats, roaches, etc.) crashed the party. There was always at least one person who would gush, "I think this is the best opening ever." Maybe the best part came after we brought in our welcoming sign and locked the door. Usually there remained bottles of wine that were only partially depleted. We treated them all as if a priest had opened them and then blessed them for a communion service. The priest, in keeping with his duty, was required to finish off the wine rather than pour it down the drain. We acted like those priests, realizing that it wasn't much of a reward for all the work.

I wondered what Gertrude Ginzer's reaction would be if I asked her to return as curator. After my experiences, I suspected it would be, "You've gotta be kidding! I found a sucker to take the job, and I'm never going to do it again." I figured I'd have to borrow some of Gertrude's lines to address another candidate for the job: "Seth (or Bob or William, or whoever), I'd like to ask a favor. There's a job you'd be perfect for." But I knew I would have to be honest about the position and say, "Would you be willing to take over as curator for the art strolls? It will mean lots of hard work, sort of like moving a locomotive from your lawn. You'll have to put up with an apathetic public, ego-driven artists, some negligent co-workers, and, occasionally, an ill-mannered visitor, with only a faint prospect of selling any art." I suspected that I wouldn't get too many takers.

However, just maybe, there might be one in our midst that needed to shore up his or her business card with the title "curator." It would allow me to get away and take a proper stroll—in the woods, during the evening, preferably on the first Friday of the month.

09
The Chili Artist

I first met Bob Butz, owner of a self-named hardware store in town, at an arts and crafts show in Maggie Valley, North Carolina, where I had set up a ten-by-ten tent so I could sell my art. He was a handsome man: tall, athletic, with an abundance of hair that made it look as if someone had overseeded his head. He had come inside my space with his wife to inspect my pieces. With a mellifluous voice that one usually hears coming from a radio DJ, he must have repeated a half dozen times the phrase, "This is the work of a true artist," or some variant of it.

At one point, his wife chimed in, "Just like you, Bob; you're an artist too."

"Is this true?" I asked, curious about what medium this robust man preferred.

"Yes, but maybe not in the exact way you'd expect. You see, in this county I'm known as the 'chili artist.' I get the name because I always win the county chili jamboree, or almost always. There was that one occasion when I was sick with the flu and my wife persuaded me that I wouldn't want to infect everybody else, though I was more than willing to give it a go anyway, and I think I disappointed a lot of people by not being there. It'd that right, Babe?"

"Yes, and you would have won, like you always do," she exuded.

"Maybe so, maybe so, but we'll never know, will we? The best I can do is try to win all the ones I can attend, including the one coming up in less than a week."

"Does anyone ever call you the 'chili king'?" I asked.

"No, never. They all know how I go about preparing each year's entry. 'Chili king' is far too common, too humdrum for what I do. All my trophies, plaques, and ribbons say 'chili artist' on them. It's a show of respect for my technique."

"I wish I could see your technique and all the awards you've won."

"Well, today is a perfect time. As I said, there's a contest this next weekend, and I'm in my 'chili artist' way of thinking. I'm seeing you in your domain as an artist; let me show my 'studio.' Why don't you swing by my house when you finish here for the day? It's only about two miles away. I'll give you directions."

Even though I knew I would be fatigued from the day outside in the show, I agreed.

If you had never heard that Bob Butz was the "Chili Artist" before you entered his house, you'd know it once you stepped into the foyer. It was a fifteen by fifteen room made smaller by heavy oak cabinets hugging the walls. Across the top of each cabinet was stretched a wide sign that said, "Bob Butz, Chili Artist." All four sides of each cabinet consisted of sliding glass doors/windows. Inside each was a formidable collection of trophies, ranging in size from two or three inches tall to a couple that could rival the Stanley Cup. There was also a battery of plaques, arranged in rows or stacked on top of each other. Filling out the rest of the space was an array of blue, red, and white ribbons, with the blue ones situated for maximum visibility. Some were mere strips with a sticker attached; others looked like giant sunflowers in bloom.

We did not leave the foyer for almost thirty minutes, during which Butz expounded in detail on each of his contests, except the ones for which he received either a white or red ribbon. If I had been more interested or less tired from my day at the show, I would have asked why, in those latter cases, his didn't measure up to some mysterious winning chili. Listening to him speak so ardently about chili contests was right up there with listening to a golfer who describes how he hit all ninety-eight strokes to win the third flight of the club championship.

To divert him finally, I asked how his competitors came up with the epithet, "chili artist," for him.

"Not to sound immodest, but you know the old saying, 'Some are born great, some achieve greatness, and some have greatness thrust upon them.' I guess I've been lucky in that my competitors have thrust greatness upon me."

"Does your chili taste better than theirs?"

"Again, not to seem immodest, but, yes, it does taste better, but that's only part of the reason I've been labeled as such. Come, let me show you my studio where I do my best work." He led me into a portion of his kitchen that ostensibly had been set aside for just his "artistry." In the middle of the counter rested a large cooking pot, labeled "Butz's Artwork." I could imagine that it carried a fair measure of intimidation at the various cook-offs. Next to it sat an artist's vase—a brush holder—except that it was filled with large wooden spoons, ladles, an assortment of knives, a whisk, a couple of tablespoons, and several smaller fractional measuring spoons. A wooden box, in which one would expect to find tubes of paint, held a large variety of herbs and spices, including black pepper, salt, cayenne, oregano, cumin, thyme, bay leaves, parsley, and garlic. Sitting next to the artist's box were bowls of chili peppers, sun-dried tomatoes, and different colored onions, plus containers of chili sauce, tomato paste, diced tomatoes, beef broth, Worcestershire sauce, and kidney beans. Off to the side stood an artist's easel, on which he had stuck printed recipes. I assumed he kept various forms of fresh meat in the refrigerator. Butz completed the tableau by donning what he called his "artist's habiliments," consisting of not a chef's hat and an apron, as one would expect, but rather an artist's smock and a black beret. He affected more traits of a stereotypical artist than I ever did as I painted. I was almost surprised not to find a couple of canvases with chili painted on them.

"Looks like you're all set," I said.

"I'd better be. The local TV station will be there giving us coverage."

After the demonstration I did not see Butz until the morning of the Jamboree. He had invited me to drop by his house again, about an hour before the contest, so I could see him putting on his final artistic touches.

He met me at the front door with desperation written over every feature. He was wringing his chili-spotted hands. His beret was missing. His smock was twisted around so that it looked more like a badly fitting hospital gown and was covered in tomato sauce, giving him the appearance of a bloodied patient who had awakened during an operation.

"What gives?" I asked.

"I've gone and done a terrible thing!"

He paused just long enough for me to speculate on what had happened: He accidentally substituted arsenic for cumin; the family dog had eaten part or all of the payload; or, perhaps, something minor, he had used dark kidney beans instead of red ones.

"I burned the chili!"

"Surely you mean just part of it. Can't some of it be salvaged?"

"No, the whole pot is ruined."

"How did you do that?"

"I had just put in the last ingredients and wanted everything to blend under a bit of high heat, when the lady next door called and said she had saved an article in the Raleigh newspaper, which I don't have a subscription to, about me and my chili. I didn't think I was gone for more than a minute or so. She asked about my chili and I guess I got carried away talking about it. At any rate, when I got back, all I had was a pot of crusted lava. This wouldn't have happened if my wife had been here, instead of traipsing off to a garden club confab."

"Can't you start over?"

"No, I don't have sufficient time, since the Jamboree begins in just over an hour, and besides, I've used up most of the ingredients I need. I was counting on doing it right the first time. I never make a mistake."

You did this time, I thought. "So I guess you'll have to withdraw," I offered.

"No can do. I've got too much at stake. People would pester me to find out why the county's 'chili artist' was withdrawing and once they found out, they'd mock me the whole next year. My hardware business would probably suffer since people come in all during the year just to see in person the 'chili artist.' And as I said a while ago, the television people will be there."

He had been hunched over as if he felt a tremendous weight on his upper back, but suddenly he stood erect and thrust his hands over his head, as if he were a referee signaling a touchdown. "I've got an idea. Maybe the day isn't lost yet. Wendy's is open for lunch already, and they have chili on their menu. It's not bad if I recall. The nearest one is only ten or fifteen minutes away. Get in the car."

"Surely you're not going to replace yours with Wendy's chili! Everyone has tasted it at some time in their life."

"Yes, but do they remember that taste? I'm betting not. Besides, sometimes an artist has to be creative." With that he roared off towards Wendy's, with me along for the ride. He still had on his sauce-stained smock, but had not taken the time to find his beret.

The next half an hour was more comical than urgent—at least for me.

When Butz arrived at Wendy's, he skipped the drive-through and went inside, immediately ordering a whole pot of chili. "We don't sell it that way," said a red-haired teenager, who looked to be too young to have a driver's license.

"Let me see the manager," Butz demanded.

"I am the manager," the boy responded with a slight degree of indignation.

"Well then, Mr. Manager, can't you figure a price for all the chili you have in your pot and sell the entire contents to me?"

"That's against our policy. We only sell it by the cup. It's a dollar fifty eight for a twelve ounce serving."

"Okay, okay, then fill up as many cups as you can."

"It'll take a few minutes, ladling a whole pot's worth into the individual cups."

"Fine, just do it as fast as you can." Butz and I watched as the manager laboriously filled fourteen cups of chili, even prolonging the process a few times by carefully wiping clean the sides of the cups. At one point he asked about the sauce stains on the "apron" Butz was wearing, who tersely told the boy that it was an artist's smock and to mind his own business.

"That's all we have."

"Great, now bag them up and let me pay. Then we'll be out of you way." The total came to $22.12 plus tax, which Butz paid before scurrying to his car. "Here, you hold the sacks," he said to me. "I don't want another accident."

"Accident!" I thought. Gabbing with a neighbor about a laudatory article in the newspaper and probably taking lots of extra time boasting about his surefire upcoming victory hardly served as the basis for an "accident." I thought how funny it would be if Butz had a fender bender on the way home, causing me to dump over the bags filled with cups of chili. But for now, he had over ten pounds of substitute chili.

Back at Butz's house, after he had chipped and scrubbed out the burnt chili from his pot and was pouring in the fourteen cups from Wendy's, I ventured to ask, "Will you add anything before you take it to the show?" hoping for even a token contribution from him.

"Maybe I should." When all the cups of Wendy's finest were in the pot, he added some parsley on top to spell out "Butz."

"That ought to make it authentic enough," he smirked. "Would you help me get it there?"

I agreed to go along if for no other reason than to see what happened at the judging. Butz straightened out his smock, but left the stains, which, he said, gave it more verisimilitude. He also found his beret.

The Jamboree was held in the county high school's gymnasium. Tables were set up on a wide arc with the cooks (or "artists," if the were cast from the same mold as Butz) standing behind their chili. The schedule called for the judges to make their rounds first and, then, after making their decisions, to allow the general public to sample the ones they desired, after which they could cast a ballot for "The People's Choice." Butz had already bragged to me that he usually won both ways. Most of the contestants were already in place when we arrived, but we still had a couple of minutes before the judging began. Suddenly, Butz leaned over to me, holding a large index card. "I've got one more favor to ask."

"What is it?"

"Well, I'm on shaky grounds here since it's not my chili," which had to be one of the world's greatest understatements. "Would you be willing to write an endorsement for it, with your signature attached? It could say something like 'Backed by an artist,' or 'Other artists love the work of a true artist,' something simple."

"What good would that do?"

"You're well known around here. Seeing your name by the chili might keep people from concentrating on the actual taste."

"But I haven't tasted it, and of course I know it's phony."

"It doesn't matter. Just your words will be enough. Your critical judgment won't count here."

"And that doesn't bother you?"

"No, why does it bother you?"

"Because it's like my going down to an art sale held in the back of a truck in the parking lot of a motel on Saturday morning and buying a fifty-nine dollar oil that has been mass produced in China, and then trying to sell it as if I had painted it."

"But don't you see, the people buying it from you are just as happy as if it were truly yours. They like the prestige; they like what they THINK is yours. People 'like' my chili because they think I did it. Phoniness doesn't count."

After a moment's hesitation while I thought over his words, I said, "I think I'll pass on this one. I'll walk back to my car. Good luck with your show." I then left, skipping all of the samples being offered. For all I knew, every one of them could have been Wendy's chili.

It came as no surprise, when I read the local paper the next day, that Butz had won both the judges' prize and the "People's Choice" award. I at least came out of the ordeal with an expanded understanding of the term "artist." Hell, there could be pancake artists, salad artists, hamburger artists out there.

I wondered what Butz would submit next year.

10
The Artist Stalker

Jeffrey Adams had often dreamed of having a fan club for his art, a group of followers that would consistently attend his shows and make repeated purchases, maybe even taking with them a half dozen of his works at a time. He fantasized about his in-box being stuffed with emails sent by a large group of satisfied customers explaining what they liked most about his art, offering also names of acquaintances they wanted to discover Jeffrey's work.

That was his dream.

The reality was that he had been forced to settle for scattered individuals who liked his work and could be counted upon to visit his display, but only a couple of times a year, not every show.

He was therefore initially elated when a mid-twenties man named Clyde Flinger appeared at three weekend shows in a row. Flinger had first introduced himself and then half shouted, "So you're the real Jeffrey Adams. I've admired your work for quite some time now. I've seen it in a bunch of locations, including banks, hospitals, and of course commercial galleries. What a privilege to meet you in person! Here, let me shake your hand." He grabbed on to Jeffrey's right hand with both of his own and did not let go until he had pumped Jeffrey's hand up and down so many times Jeffrey began to think Flinger had mistaken him for a water pump. "With your black pants and black turtleneck, you look just like what I imagined you would—a real artist."

To back up his lauding, he actually bought a landscape at each of the three shows, two photographs, and a watercolor painting. "This is great," Flinger pronounced with each purchase. "It means so much to me to actually buy something directly from you!" Flinger seemed to get more exuberant with each passing week, saying almost the same thing each time he bought a work, essentially, causing Jeffrey to suspect his sincerity. While he was excited about having a true fan, Jeffrey was just a bit put off by Flinger's excessive excitement and aggression.

It reminded him of a time when he was teaching an introduction to watercolor painting class at the local college and, through a mistake on the registrar's part, had ended up with twice the number of students the course could accommodate (thirty instead of fifteen). He met all thirty the first day and then took the problem to the department head, who contacted another artist named Ben Johnson, who was willing to take half of the class. "How shall we divide them?" Johnson asked.

"How about I take the first half of the alphabetically arranged list and you the others?" was Jeffrey's suggestion, which Johnson quickly agreed to.

What Jeffrey failed to mention was that on the first day of the class, one member established himself as someone Jeffrey did not want to put up with for a whole semester. The student had a cloying personality that demanded too much personal attention and one who blustered far too loudly, almost to the point of braying. His name was Thomas Thompson, so obviously he was not on Jeffrey's half of the list. Jeffrey had felt some regret about the dirty trick, particularly when Ben Johnson stopped him after about the fifth day of classes and pleaded, "I'll trade my best looking and brightest student for the worst two you have if you will also take Thomas Thompson in the deal." Jeffrey rejected the offer, claiming that he had already established "rapport" with each member of his class.

Clyde Flinger almost gave him the same uneasiness that Thompson had, but at least he bought art.

Flinger did not appear at the next show, which came three weeks later, but as Jeffrey was setting up for the next show after that, some fifteen minutes or so before the official opening time of 10 am, there appeared Flinger, who immediately delivered a detailed explanation about why he had skipped the previous show, something having to do with a broken down car and failure to borrow his aunt's van. Jeffrey listened as best he could while struggling to finish setting up, possibly offending Flinger a couple of times when he forgot details about the cause of the problem and had asked Flinger to repeat some of his information. Flinger looked decidedly hurt when Jeffrey said, "I'm sorry about your car, but you certainly don't have to be at every show I do."

Flinger replied with a pout, "But now that I've met you, I want to see any new work you've done. If I miss a show, you may sell something I've not seen."

"That's unlikely, but I'm glad you like my work," Jeffrey said aloud, while entertaining doubts which he kept to himself. "Well, I'm going to have to excuse myself and finish setting up. It's almost time for the show to open. Why don't you take a tour of the booths and see what the other artists have to offer."

"All right, but I'm sure I won't like theirs as much as yours."

"Take your time; I'm not going anywhere." Jeffrey noticed that as Flinger moved from booth to booth down the row, he continually looked back toward Jeffrey, waving when he caught Jeffrey's eye. He was relieved when Flinger was out of sight, but he had an uncomfortable feeling that Flinger was still watching him, and sure enough, while talking to a customer, he happened to look at a booth a good fifty yards away and spotted Flinger inside it, watching him from behind some pottery. Flinger ducked down when it was clear Jeffrey had seen him and did not reappear for several minutes.

When Flinger did return to Jeffrey's booth, he was even more effusive about Jeffrey's art than before. Jeffrey briefly considered asking what it was about his works that Flinger liked, but he did not really want to get into a discussion of aesthetics with someone who was increasingly giving him the creeps.

Flinger hung around for almost two more hours, either acting as an erstwhile agent/broker for Jeffrey's art (or barker), loudly announcing to potential customers why they should make purchases there, or sitting in Jeffrey's chair and making comments as if he were a director of a documentary film about Jeffrey's art. During the two hours he bought another photograph from Jeffrey, but made Jeffrey regret the sale by using the picture as a prop. "Look, folks, at this lovely piece I just bought." Jeffrey was sure Flinger had driven away more sales than he had given Jeffrey with his one purchase.

Jeffrey's relief came in the form of a volunteer, whose purpose was to watch an artist's booth while the artist took a bathroom or snack break. "I could do that for you," whined Flinger.

"No, that's okay. These people know just what they're supposed to do, including taking credit cards." Jeffrey pulled from his pocket a predetermined variety of bills to use for change in a cash transaction and gave it to the volunteer. "See you, Clyde, maybe at another show." Jeffrey hoped this sign off would make clear that their artist/admirer stint was over for the day.

It almost didn't. Jeffrey made his way to the Portajohns, followed by Flinger, who took up a position nearby as if he were a prison warden keeping an eye on a chain-gang member. Fortunately for Jeffrey, the Portajohns had slotted airways at the top, which made it possible for him to watch Flinger. The second Flinger was distracted—by a mini-parade of clowns—Jeffrey slipped out and then took a circuitous route that prevented Flinger from seeing him. He swung by the food court and ordered a sandwich, taking longer than he normally would. He finally returned to his booth, where he thanked the volunteer, glad to find no Flinger. Without Flinger's interference, he made several sales during the afternoon.

He would have preferred forgetting about Flinger during the month before his next show, but Flinger made that impossible by sending numerous emails, including one in which he cryptically noted that he had a "big surprise" for Jeffrey at the next show. When 10 am came and went without Flinger, Jeffrey felt a slight surge of hope that Flinger would not appear.

No such luck. Just after 11 am here he came, announcing his presence from about five booths away, hollering out, "I bet you thought I wasn't coming." He was carrying a large folder. When he arrived at the booth, he first complained, "Did you know that they're charging customers three dollars to get in this time? You'd think that they would want as many buyers as possible. I wouldn't have paid if your name hadn't been on the list of artists. But I wanted to show you my surprise. Are you ready?"

"I guess so," Jeffrey answered with as much enthusiasm as he could muster. "What's in the folder?"

Flinger opened it to reveal four or five watercolor paintings and a collection of unmatted photographs, Jeffrey first looked at the photographs. "I've been using an i-Phone to take the pictures," Flinger said with pride. "I think you can get ones as good as those done with a professional camera. Plus I have a pretty decent printer."

Though the quality of the printer—and by extension the iPhone used to take the picture—was impressive, the pictures themselves were clearly the work of someone who had no sense whatsoever of arrangement, spacing, or lighting. Any feature a good photographer must keep in mind was missing in the collection Flinger presented. It included a picture of Flinger's feet, taken while he was standing up looking down.; a picture of the front half of a Chihuahua; a blurry picture of a tree that had no distinguishing features; an up close shot of a kitchen sink; and an almost not bad picture of an umbrella standing in the corner of a room; and then a picture of a deer taken from no more than fifteen feet away. For the most part the pictures reminded Jeffrey of the pictures taken by Dustin Hoffman's character in *Rainman*.

"You're right about iPhones. You probably can get just as good a photo as you would with the right equipment." He didn't want to sound as ironic as he actually meant to be. "Stay with it, and you'll get better. What's the story on the deer?"

"I like to take pictures of animals. I also like to hunt, particularly deer. There's a place in Texas that has a confinement for keeping wild animals for hunters. I wanted to get a photograph of the one I wanted to shoot, so I took the picture of it the day before. The photograph usually sits below the stuffed head of the deer in my den. I brought it today because I think it's one of my best."

"Was the deer that close to you when you shot it?" Jeffrey asked in amazement.

"Oh, no, that wouldn't have been very sporting on my part. No, I nailed him from about fifty yards. I really like his color. Now tell me what you think of my paintings."

Jeffrey was hard pressed to give a legitimate critical comment since the paintings were even more amateurish than the photographs, though the word "amateurish" probably was the wrong one to use since it connoted at least stage one of progress toward something professional. Most of them were versions of the photographs he had taken, but there was also one of a face—presumably Flinger's own—that was particularly disturbing, with eyes too big for the face, lips drooping, neck too long. Jeffrey wondered if it was a product of Flinger's self-image or just more bad art.

He searched through his mental critical menu to come up with a term to give Flinger's collection, discarding "dismal," "disgusting," and "depressing," and settling on the all-purpose "interesting."

"Do you think I could sell any of them? I've got lots more, mostly

Errata

Publication page—"Artist Tales" should be "Artists' Tales"
p. 10, 3rd parag.,line 9—drop"ly" from "eventually"
p. 23, 4th parag.—inconsistent indentation
p. 34, 1st parag., 3r line—"Bert" should be "Burt"
p. 35, next to last parag., 7th line—needs "he" after "as if"
p. 37, 2nd parag., 3rd line--needs "as" before "if"
p, 47, end of 2nd parag.—needs period after "weapon"
p. 49, 2nd line—needs space between "as" and "Forest"
p. 50, 2nd line—needs "on" before "my paintings"
p. 50, 3rd line—"line should be "lined"
p. 57, 3rd parag.—needs "was" in sentence beginning "Yes"
p. 71, 2nd parag., 7th line—"trees" should be "plants"
pp 78-81—inconsistency indentations
p. 103, fifth parag., 3rd line—i-Phone" should be "iPhone"
p. 105, next to last parag., 3rd line—"painting" should be "paintings"
p. 106, 5th parag., 3rd line—"of " before "Flingers" should be "on"
p. 107, next to last parag., 3rd line—"painting" should be "paintings"
p. 108, 2nd parag, 1st line—"if' needs to be "is" before "a rip off"
p. 110, 2nd parag., 4th line—"back pack" should be "backpack"
p. 110, 5th parag., 3rd line—"back pack" should be "backpack"
p. 110, last line—needs a space between comma and "at least"
p. 112, 1st parag., 4th line—"back pack" should be "backpack"

landscapes like yours, plus a bunch of animals, some of which I killed shortly after taking the pictures."

"Gee, I don't know, Clyde. It's hard to predict the public's taste. The trick is first getting through the jurying process."

"What's that?"

The safeguard that keeps junk like this out of shows and galleries, Jeffrey thought. "You have to submit samples of your work to a committee for the show or owner of the gallery, who decide if your work meets their standards. It's pretty competitive."

"Wow, I didn't know that," Flinger responded, as if Jeffrey had just given him the secret to instant success. "Did you have to do that?"

"At the beginning I did, but as I got into more and more galleries and shows, I got invited to be in other ones."

Just then some customers came into the tent. "You'll have to excuse me, Clyde; I need to get to work. See you around."

"Can I get a picture of you before I leave?" Flinger asked, as he pulled out his cell phone.

Though he suddenly got visions of his head mounted on Flinger's den wall next to the deer, Jeffrey agreed.

Flinger took the picture while Jeffrey still had these morbid thoughts in his head. "You didn't smile," he said. "Let's do another."

This time Jeffrey managed to pull up a fake smile, which seemed good enough for Flinger. "Thanks for the advice," he said, as he began gathering his photographs and painting into his folder, leaving Jeffrey asking himself, "What advice? All I have done is dispense some information."

"One more thing and I'll be off. Since I have some of my work here, are you interested in trading? I'd love to swap any of mine for one of your photographs of the covered bridge."

"Thanks for the offer, Clyde, but I need all of the ones I brought. I have a definite plan that I would like to stick to. Maybe some other time."

Flinger looked hurt, but finished putting away his pictures, and then he was gone.

A month passed before Jeffrey's next show, during which time he painted some watercolor landscapes and made several treks into the back country or up mountains to take photographs. He also visited the galleries in which his works hung, to replenish the stock. In three of them, the owners came up with essentially the same words: "Do you know someone named Flinger? He comes in here, but only wants to see your work. Sometimes he takes pictures of your work. He says you wouldn't mind since you two are the best of friends. He hung around in the gallery long enough to make a pest of himself as he directed customers to you work. Now he wants to bring some of his work for jurying. He said you would approve."

To each of the curators he had the same response: "No, I don't approve, but it's not up to me to say." He was confident that no reputable curator/gallery owner would ever consider any of Flinger's work.

At the end of the month recess, Jeffrey was setting up for his next show when he suddenly felt a hand on his shoulder. It was Flinger, dressed just like Jeffrey in all black. Jeffrey started to comment of Flinger's choice, but decided not to, wishing to avoid drawing attention to any connection between the two of them. "Oh, hi, Clyde," he mumbled in a flat voice. "How's it going?"

"Good and bad. I've missed attending any show with your work in it, but I've been able to see it in galleries. I wanted to keep your images fresh in my mind."

"Oh, why's that?"

"Just because I like them so much. You do what I want to do. Have you brought any new works?"

"Yes, all of these over here. Take a look while I finish setting up."

'Splendid!" Jeffrey cringed since Flinger's word was one of his least favorites. At least he didn't amplify it into "splendiferous."

Flinger stayed for almost half an hour in Jeffrey's booth, studying mainly his new works. Jeffrey wasn't completely sure, but he thought he saw Flinger taking pictures of them with his cell phone, while pretending to talk on it. He had allowed Flinger to take pictures before so he didn't make any issue of it.

Flinger left after delivering his usual battery of false-sounding compliments and trying to sway customers to buy from this man "who's the best around." To Jeffrey's relief, he did not return.

As a matter of fact, he did not see Flinger at any of the next three shows spread over the next two months. It was only by accident that he did finally meet Flinger, but not at his booth or in a gallery. He had decided to take a week off after the three shows in a row. He just happened to be in a town where a show was taking place, so, having some free time on his hands, he decided to check it out. He relished the thought of looking at the works of other artists without having to rush back to his own booth.

About half way through his stroll, he suddenly halted. He was standing face to face with a grinning Flinger, who now had his own booth with approximately a dozen paintings and a dozen photographs hanging.

Most of the pieces looked like Jeffrey's own work, except done in an elementary style. "Oh, hi," Flinger said sheepishly. "Are you in this show? I didn't see you listed among the participating artists."

"No, I skipped this one. What are you doing here? How did you get in?" Jeffrey asked in disbelief.

"Someone dropped out at the last minute, and I happened to be in the right place at the right time. My cousin Benny is one of the organizers. He told me I could be here as long as I didn't try to resell painting or photographs I bought from Walmart or some such place."

"I can't believe it," Jeffrey said. "The jurying process is supposed to be very stringent at these shows."

"Are you saying my work isn't good enough?" Flinger asked with a heretofore unseen boldness.

"It could be if it were really your work. Most of what I see if a rip-off of mine."

"What's the matter? Can't stand a little competition?"

"I don't mind competition, but I do mind plagiarism."

"I didn't copy your art. Mine is quite different from yours." He did have a point, Jeffrey had to admit. Even though the paintings were attempts to emulate his, they came out all wrong, with spacing and arrangement off, the colors different, the overall effect much less pleasing. And most of the photographs, while being attempts to match Jeffrey's originals, were clumsily done, with the wrong light, peculiar spacing, and a lack of focus. The other photographs were the same ones Flinger had brought to Jeffrey's booth in a folder a few weeks back, including the slaughtered deer. At least they could be considered original. Jeffrey was pretty sure no one else at the show took pictures of animals they intended to kill.

Doubly disturbed by Flinger's being in the show and plagiarizing some of his work, Jeffrey suddenly lost all interest in being there. Without any of the usual departure amenities, he headed for the nearest exit.

Two weeks later, he was setting up for another show. He had checked the roster and found no listing for Flinger, but within approximately fifteen minutes Flinger appeared.

"No pictures, if you don't mind," Jeffrey said sarcastically.

"Oh, I don't need them. I'm doing quite well with my own now. I sold a bunch at that show you visited. It seems that people enjoy the naturalness of my work, both the paintings and the photographs. With my cell phone I'm always equipped. My customers particularly like my pictures of animals. They go crazy when they see pictures of the ones I shot and mounted."

After Flinger left, Jeffrey pondered the question of how many Flingers were out there, glutting art shows with cell phone art—and bad art at that. And he thought about his own part in the process of unleashing a Flinger on the art community.

He also thought about the people at shows like this one, who bought Flinger's art. What kind of patron would buy a Flinger? Who were the judges that would let Flinger display his works at a show? Was there something in Flinger's art that Jeffrey didn't see? Was his own art really better than Flinger's? He began to call into question his own notion of aesthetics.

He shuddered at the thought of being in the same show with Flinger sometime in the future. Would visitors equate his art with Flinger's since the two of them were both set up? He could only hope that the people coming to the shows would have some discrimination, but he wasn't convinced that they would.

He concluded that all he could do was depict what he personally liked. If buyers preferred a Flinger or a piece hanging in a grocery store over his, then, so be it, but he vowed to be more alert for the Flingers of the art world and to avoid contact with them—if that were ever possible.

11
Forest Service

Stella Longstar gasped, then sprang from the rock that had served as her seat, almost dropping the canvas on which she had been painting. This was all due to the sudden appearance of a hiker on the trail she had been sitting next to.

There was really nothing for her to be alarmed about. The hiker was an ordinary looking young man, with a face like John Denver's, probably in his early twenties, wearing tan cargo hiking shorts and a t-shirt with a picture of U2 on the front and toting a dark green back pack.

Momentarily flustered, she demanded, "Where'd you come from?"

"Wayah Bald," he stammered. "Is there something wrong? Am I not supposed to be on this trail?" he asked, obviously acknowledging the fact that she was wearing a Forest Service uniform.

"No, it's all right. It's open to the public. You just startled me, that's all. I was a bit engrossed in doing a . . . finishing a project." She said this as she slipped her canvas, brushes, and paints into her own back pack, which had been lying at her feet.

Emboldened by her answer, at least to the point he no longer stammered, he said, "I noticed that you were painting a picture of the mountain ranges to our west here. Are you doing it for the Forest Service?"

"Uh, yes. Yes, that's it." She did not want to admit that she was stealing company time by doing what she loved to do more than anything–painting pictures of the landscape or of spiders, which she found fascinating with their weaving and designs.

"Do you ever take a photograph of the scene you want to depict and then work on the painting at home?"

"No, I prefer the 'plein aire' experience when I do my paintings."

"What's that?"

"It's simply the technique of painting outdoors, on site. It works for me since I feel as though I can transfer the smells and feel of the earth and trees into my paintings."

"Sounds like a perfect technique for capturing the beauty of a place such as this. Well, I'd better be off. I need to reach the trail hut at Grassy Bald by dark. Nice talking with you. Sorry if I interrupted anything."

Stella was not sorry to see him go. One of the main attractions of her job with the Forest Service–in addition to providing her with ample subjects to paint–was the opportunity to be alone in nature. She was assigned several miles of trail to monitor and maintain, so she spent much of her time hiking with only trees, bushes, and spiders for company. This gave her opportunities to stop and paint. She justified these "time outs" to herself by considering her very modest salary.

Most of the time, she could hear a person coming along the trail, especially on a quiet, windless day. People talk, sing, scrape, dislodge rocks. If they were ordinary hikers, like the one today, she usually set her work aside until they had passed by. They didn't bother her. All she was concerned about was getting caught by a co-worker doing what basically equaled an office worker's playing video games during work hours.

Usually, her co-workers made it easy for her by calling out her name from afar, in which case she stowed her materials in her backpack, or, if pressed for time, hid them behind a tree. The latter had precipitated one awkward moment with a worker named Gene, who, after a short conversation, said, "Grab your back pack and come on; I'm headed the same way you are." She was forced into pretending to start out with him, then, after hiking about a hundred yards, to ask for moment of privacy, during which she returned to her painting spot, gathered her goods from behind a tree, and placed them in her backpack, without stopping for the implied pee.

However, she had been caught twice with her guard completely down by other Forest Service workers. On each occasion, fortunately with different discoverers, she had weaseled out by claiming a semi-work related reason behind her painting: "I like to capture a specific mountain topography" or "I like to record the direction of the sun relative to the trail, all for future reference," though she did not say how she would ever use this information. Each time, she had spoken with the sheepishness of a young teenaged girl caught smoking by her mom, but the co-workers had not reported her dereliction.

Gradually, Stella became known as the "mystery painter," an epithet bestowed by fellow workers who, believing that she returned to selected sites on her own time, admired her productivity. "We're all amazed that you can find the time to do so many paintings," gushed a ranger named June. "How do you do it?"

"It does keep me busy, but I'd do anything for art," Stella said, evading the question.

The title also fit her in that she was reluctant to sell any of her paintings. "Why don't you?" quizzed her cousin Zelda. "I'm sure you could use the extra money."

Stella ignored this implied slur on her salary. She was used to indulging Zelda because Zelda often visited Stella's father, Robert Longstar, when Stella could not, a situation created by the fact that Robert and Zelda lived in a city two hours away from where Stella lived. "I'm afraid that my works might fall in the hands of people who don't share my passion for nature, who would never feel the 'plein aire' experience I felt when I painted the pieces," Stella responded. "Not to mention I don't trust viewers to discover my focal point, my use of negative space, or my balancing of tones."

"How about some of your paintings of spiders? I'd bet they'd sell."

"Oh, no, they're the last thing I would let go. I doubt seriously if anybody could grasp a spider's poisonous beauty like I do."

"I do understand how personal they are to you." Zelda knew that the spiders were the one part of the settings Stella physically took home with her, particularly black widows and brown recluses, which Stella had carefully stowed in small jars. She wanted to say more on the subject, but shelved the topic and said instead, "I just think you should get something in return for your art."

"Oh, I definitely do," Stella nearly shouted.

It really did not matter to Stella that she sold very few of her works. Despite Zelda's jabs, she made enough from the Forest Service to fulfill her needs. She saved money by renting a small apartment, with no view of trees or mountains; and she drove a nine-year old Honda Civic, which passed inspection each year only after a lot of haggling and Stella's displaying the best of her feminine wiles. She was a beauty for sure, with long, naturally wavy hair, a figure that made even the standard issue Park Service uniform look sexy, boots included. How much that beauty played a part in the passed inspections is hard to say; it all could have happened anyway, even if Stella had looked like a box of cereal in the uniform, since a government uniform carries its own kind of persuasion.

There was one thing she did not scrimp on: her art supplies. She still bought the best of everything: the best sable brushes, heavyweight cotton canvas, Belgian linen, Old Holland oils, Golden acrylics, DaVinci watercolors, expensive frames. She felt that the scenes she painted deserved optimum presentation. Of course all of these expenses seemingly did not leave her with a lot of extra money, as Zelda often reminded her.

What Zelda did not know, and a practice that puzzled Stella's co-workers, was that Stella would occasionally show up with an expensive piece of pottery, woodworking, or quilting she had bought and request that everyone (except Zelda) help her "celebrate" the new acquisition. This celebration included fine wine and heavy hors d'oeuvres. In answer to the question of how she could afford all this, she blithely answered, "Oh, I sold a couple of commissioned paintings." Coincidentally, she had spent several days with her eighty-one year old father, who she had recently proclaimed was doing quite well financially and physically (except for allergies, supposedly aggravated by mosquito bites).

Soon, however, everything returned to normal, with Stella living a Spartan lifestyle. This became the pattern for Stella. She would live frugally for a while, painting sparingly using what material she could scrape together, occasionally accepting an invitation to join another artist who was willing to buy her lunch. She made no mention of exactly what role her father played in her life, but every month or two she did offer the excuse that she could not attend some event sponsored by the Arts Council or the Forest Service because she had to visit her father, after which she would repeat her generous spending and offer invitations to her lavish parties. Most of the attendees figured that she simply had her pride and did not want to come across as a mooching daughter.

When asked why her father never came to visit her, she tersely answered, "Oh, he's much too fragile to travel," totally contradicting what she had said earlier about his well being.

One day she approached her boss and said, "I need two weeks off."

"What's the problem?" he asked.

"My father is not well. He needs me. You can take the two weeks out of my vacation time, or, if I have to, I'll forfeit my pay for those days."

"The latter won't be necessary. We can take it out of your vacation time. What's wrong with him? I was under the impression that he was doing well."

"I'd rather not discuss it."

With that, she was gone for two weeks. When she returned, she told everyone, "The doctors think he's just giving out. They don't give him much of a chance." She received several shows of sympathy, in response to which she said, with tears welling in her eyes, "He's my best friend. I do love him so."

Two days later she announced that he had died. "I should have been there," she lamented.

"Will there be a burial service?" her boss asked.

"No, I'm going to have his body cremated so I can keep his ashes as a reminder of what a great man he was. I'll do that just as soon as some legal matters are taken care of."

While her father's body lay in the morgue, Stella acted as if she truly had all the money she could want. She went on a shopping excursion, buying even more expensive paintings and superior equipment for her own use. She even made arrangements to rent a larger apartment, one that gave her a studio, which she immediately used to touch up some of her "plein aire" pieces, as well as paint nude self portraits. She also bought a new all-wheel vehicle, claiming that it could more easily get her to remote areas.

In addition, she requested that she be given half-time duties, so she could "get through her grief." This allowed her to delve deeply into the obscurity of the forest, away from people, especially those who asked lots of questions about the death of her father. Incidentally, she stopped collecting spiders. When asked why, she responded, "I don't need them anymore."

Most of her fellow artists and workers simply accepted the notion that she had inherited a large sum of money from her father's estate and that she was reluctant to talk about it. But there was one person who was less than satisfied with the whole process. This was Zelda, who had attended to Stella's father far more than Stella had and had been more alarmed at his downward spiral than anyone else, including Stella.

Keeping Stella out of the picture, Zelda convinced the coroner to investigate the body thoroughly, thus creating the delay in cremation that Stella had alluded to with her co-workers. It did not take long until the coroner discovered the plethora of spider bites that Stella had claimed were the work of mosquitoes. His first utterance after sighing and tsk-tsking was, "We must have mosquitoes that are as big as bumblebees and more poisonous than rattlesnakes."

In rapid succession, the process went like this: The coroner took several blood samples from the body, then informed the sheriff of his findings, who immediately called the Head Ranger at the Forest Service office, asked for the whereabouts of one Stella Longstar, was told that she had gone hiking to paint pictures deep in the forest, and was told to contact the local sheriff, who after hearing the whole story started a man hunt (woman hunt, or artist hunt). It took three days before one of the sworn deputies came upon her gazing at a painting she apparently had just finished, which she was now comparing to the original scene. She did not put up any resistance. She had too much pride to make an ugly scene.

When she arrived at the courthouse in the back of the deputy's police car, she was inundated by questions from the press. Her only comment was, "I'd do anything for art, and so would my father. It just so happened that I was more purposeful. He did his best, but I needed more."

"But why did you use spider venom?" one asked.

"As I said, I would do anything for art. This time art did a little something for me."

When Zelda learned about Stella's arrest, her only comment was, "She'll have a lot harder time doing 'plein aire' paintings in a jail cell."

12
An Artist's Heaven

Tyler Davidson knew that he had died. He was jogging on the shoulder of a rural highway that he had chosen for its dearth of traffic and for its scenic beauty: lots of maples, oaks, hickories, and birches in full fall color, rapidly flowing streams, rustic barns, and hills that dipped and rolled, a place he had often chosen for doing paintings. What nailed him, he thought, was either an SUV or a pick-up truck, coming fast down the shoulder from behind him, thus ending his career as an artist. What had the driver been thinking? Was he transfixed by the scenery? The whole catastrophe was over in a second.

The next thing he knew he was being guided by a timeless figure, who introduced himself as Gabriel, a psychopomp, a guide for the dead. He led Tyler to a partially open set of gates, and then with the parting words, "Wait here," vanished into the air. After he was gone, in a state of wonder, Tyler considered the scene in front of him. If he were truly dead, then, by all accounts, he should be standing before the pearly (or golden) gates of heaven, waiting for St. Peter. These gates were anything but pearly or golden. They were made from rustic wooden rails, covered by honeysuckle vines and connected to a split rail fence that ran off into the horizon both right and left. If he hadn't been dead, he would have liked to do a painting of the bucolic scene.

Before long, an old man, who looked a lot like the painter Renoir, ambled up, carrying a large folder that could have been a ledger. He stood still for several moments, eyeing Tyler quietly. Tyler was not sure who should be doing the talking. He finally decided to take the lead. "I'm Tyler Davidson, and I think I'm dead."

"I know who you are, and, yes, you are dead. Bad business back there by the road. I'm St. Luke, the patron saint of artists. You can call me Luke if you'd like. I'm not big on ceremony. I'm to be your judge and jury, so to speak."

"What happened to St. Peter? By tradition, he's the one who does this."

"Don't put too much faith in tradition. It can lead you astray. Now, let's get down to cases. What do you have to say about your life?"

Thinking that his religious life was at issue here, Tyler blurted out, "I tried several different religions or denominations, mostly Christian ones, hoping to discover some viable guiding principles that would lead to eternal life in heaven."

St. Luke lay down the folder, a slight smile on his face. "That's interesting. Why don't you tell me about some of them."

"Well, being from the South, I first tried the Southern Baptists, but I wasn't too crazy about their attitude of inequality between husband and wife. And it seemed that they met too many times a week–Sunday morning, Sunday evening, Wednesday evening, and that doesn't include all the televised church services. It wore me out. Plus, they shortchanged the congregation in the wine-tasting ceremony, what they tabbed as the Lord's Supper. They called it wine, but it was really just watered down grape juice, and in one case I suspected it was grape Kool-Aid. And I didn't like the way they demanded a tenth of everyone's income, what they called a 'tithe,' and they were talking gross, not net, but then were so stingy about helping the poor, particularly through welfare programs.

by Joseph Meigs

The clincher was their ticket to heaven seemed awfully vague—all that about 'accepting Jesus as your personal savior.' It seemed that just about anyone could get into heaven if they so-called 'repented,' or 'found Jesus,' even if they were hardened criminals about to be executed. I wanted something a bit more exclusive."

"Did you try others?" St. Luke asked.

"You bet. I tried the Methodists, but they pulled the same trick with the grape juice. And about the time I was getting accustomed to a particular pastor, they replaced him, citing some policy about moving their ministers around. Basically, I was suspicious of any denomination whose name was based upon the early founders' penchant for having a strict method in their worship."

"So I joined with the Presbyterians for a while, but got bogged down with the same indoctrination as that found with the Baptists and Methodists, emphasizing the authority of the Scriptures, and the possibility of getting to heaven only through Jesus and his 'Grace,' a concept I was never quite clear on. And I wasn't sure I wanted to be affiliated with a denomination founded by John Calvin, who believed that God willed eternal damnation for some and salvation for others. Predestination didn't seem fair."

"And the Lutherans?" Luke asked.

"The Lutherans also believe in predestination, but modify it with no one being predestined to hell, which seems a bit contradictory. But what bugged me most was that, like many other Christian denominations, they still insist that we believe in the death and resurrection of Christ."

St. Luke was still smiling. "Go on, please."

"The worst were the various evangelical or charismatic movements, including the Holy Rollers. I couldn't imagine getting into heaven based upon all the shouting, talking in tongues, and inspired fits that served as part of their 'profession of faith.' And most of them couldn't keep any kind of division between politics and religion. I heard ministers actually claim that God had chosen the right candidate for election, and he, the pastor, was there to tell the congregation which one that was. They didn't seem very tolerant of opposing points of view. And it showed up also in their inability to separate religion and education."

"Did you have a look at the Mormons?"

"Yes, but they annoyed me in that they were another denomination that in effect says, 'We've got the right doctrines and all others have wrong doctrines.' Plus I didn't like their restrictions on caffeine. I was also bothered by their history of polygamy. However, they had a nice temple and impressive music done by the Mormon Tabernacle Choir. I bought one of their albums."

"How about Roman Catholicism or its offshoot the Episcopalians?"

"Catholicism seemed to try to make everybody feel guilty, emphasizing the likelihood of spending a long time in either Hell or Purgatory, plus they were way too conservative in social matters, particularly about birth and choosing partners, taking on an absolutism and authoritarianism that disturbed me greatly. Another annoyance was the pre-programmed services, contained in books on the back of the pews. I could have stayed at home and read the service by myself, but even that would not have altered the repetitiveness of it. Plus they overdid their decor something fierce. I've never seen such gaudy stuff. I felt like I was attending services in some self-absorbed Egyptian king's palace. And all that scandal involving priests and young boys did not exactly instill confidence in me."

"And the Episcopalians weren't a whole lot better than the Catholics, maybe even acting stuffier—except when they turned evangelical. I got a good chuckle when a well dressed Episcopalian couple 'witnessed' to me by getting down on their knees at a busy intersection in town to pray for my soul. I thought for sure they were going to speak in tongues like the Holy Rollers."

St. Luke's smile began to broaden.

"Together, these two denominations seem to have the greatest number of so-called authority figures–popes, cardinals, archbishops, bishops, priests, etc. (who often wear funny hats and what appears to be shawls or blankets)–and they both require a lifetime's worth of bowing and kneeling. I was sore every Monday after going to the services of either denomination. And, in both cases, I didn't like having to drink communion wine out of the same cup that dozens of others were using, many of whom were coughing and sneezing. The minister or priest wiping the lip of the 'vessel' just wasn't very reassuring. At least it involved real wine, which put them one up on lots of other Christian denominations."

"Did any non-Christian religions interest you and give you answers about eternity?"

"Not really. I was turned off by some of the same concepts and behavior I found in Christianity–the most vocal people becoming the spokesperson for the mass of followers, who would do whatever the leader directed them to do; hierarchies of authority with a chain of command, all claiming some superiority over the average Joe who wants to worship his god; lots of rules, commandments, and 'thou shalt not's'; and lots of turf wars."

"Which ones did you try, and what did you specifically object to in each?"

"Well, let's see. Islam contends that our purpose is to love and serve God. I'm troubled by the word 'serve' when it applies to any relationship I have with another being. Plus, again, I'm bothered by any religion that claims that it should be universal and its scripture, the Qur'an, is the final word of God. I like diversity and choice. Also, they forbid alcohol and pork products. I like my barbeque sandwich and a beer too much."

"Hinduism was just too complicated, with too many rituals, ceremonies, and different gods. I think a person needs to start out early in the Hindu religion, rather than try to 'just pick it up' later in life. Also, I didn't like the pressure that their notion of karma put on me. I was self conscious about everything I did, wondering if I was creating good karma and how I was determining my fate. I didn't want to make a mistake and get reincarnated as an undesirable."

"Did you check out the Hare Krishnas?"

"Oh, yes, but they didn't appeal to me because I'm not big on chanting mantras and because I'm not keen on a religion that requires you to eat no meat or eggs, drink no caffeine–like the Mormons–and have sex only to produce children. Plus, when I think of a Hare Krishna, I get images of airports and body length Snuggies."

"I suppose you looked at Judaism."

"Yes, but I found it to be another religion that demands strict adherence to certain laws and commandments, as revealed in their scripture, the Torah. And as you can probably guess by now, it's not my nature to follow directives laid down hundreds or even thousands of years ago by the 'authorities.'"

"There were lots of others I studied, including Buddhism, which like other religions, could be traced back to the teachings of one 'enlightened' being, who shared his own personal beliefs that became the mainstay of a whole movement. They scared me with the possibility of giving up my conventional life and taking up a lot of devotional practices, even becoming monastic."

"I can see your point."

"I'm not sure if it counts as a complete religion or an offshoot of Hinduism, but I did find something I liked in Pantheism, which, as you know, posits that God broke into all the pieces of creation, so in effect all things are parts of God and therefore have a kind of beauty. But, heck, I thought something like that as an artist, particularly after reading Whitman's *Song of Myself*."

"After a while all the religions started to blend together to the point that I found fault with all of them collectively. I tried to read their adopted scriptures, but never got a clear idea of how to get to Heaven. I even read literary versions of the quest for Heaven, such as *Piers Plowman*, *Pilgrims Progress*, and *Everyman*, hoping to pick up some ideas that I might have missed, but they did not give me any new enlightenment. So I guess I blew it–disappointed God by not finding the true path to Heaven. I guess I don't qualify to get in."

St. Luke's smile now became a full-throated laughter, creating waves of rolling sound off into the distance. "On the contrary, my son, not only have you not blown it, you may be over-qualified for entry here."

"How come?"

"Let me explain. First of all, Heaven is only for artists, in all their different shapes and forms, the beings that used their time to create things of beauty. By rejecting all the structure and following of rules, you opened the door to be inventive, creative."

"But doesn't God demand that we lead a moral life, accept Jesus, bathe in the Ganges, get baptized, dwell in a monastery, or some such, in order to enter Heaven?"

"Think about how God is initially represented in the Hebrew Old Testament, as well as in most other scriptures, as the supreme creator, the great model for you and others to strive for creativity yourself. Think of God's portfolio: the earth, the sun, the stars, the Garden of Eden, which would still be beautiful if it weren't for those self-centered clowns, Adam and Eve. And the bonus for anyone who is allowed in is that it's not very crowded."

"How about the traditional features we were taught to expect: the pearly gates, the streets paved in gold?"

"Please, give God some credit. Do you actually believe that a being that could create rhododendrons, waterfalls, and giant redwoods would want such gaudy décor in Heaven? Besides it would be a waste of a useful metal. No, God wanted things simple. Thoreau was one of the great P.R. men for heaven with his notion of simplicity."

"Is there any point in any of the religions then?"

"Well, as you yourself already noticed, they have produced some great music, in addition to art and architecture. And somebody religious ought to get credit for the lyricism found in the scriptures: the songs, the poetry, the verses that were passed down orally through the ages, composed for easier memorization. Plus, the various scriptures contain lots of stories with multiple layers of meaning, filled with symbols and representations, which unfortunately get overlooked by the literalists."

"What's that folder you've got there? Is it a ledger of my deeds, like the 'Book of Count' in *Everyman*?"

"Oh, no, nothing like that. It's actually a mini-portfolio of all your art work. I particularly like your watercolors of barns and cabins. Off to the left we have a section of constructions you've never seen. Maybe one or more of them will inspire you. If they don't suit you, God has created a multitude of other settings for art, including inspirations for some modern art. That's what you get to do in heaven—create new art with lots of positives and none of the negatives."

"What positives do you mean?"

"You'll be sharing an uncrowded place populated with people like yourself, who, while living on earth, wrote poetry or a song after seeing a beautiful woman, rather than buying a box of chocolates, who wove a beautiful basket no one had ever seen before; who leaped out of a car to photograph a sunset. They'll give, along with God, their views and critiques, helping you with lots of feedback. They're the best audience you could ever want for your art."

"What were the negatives you were alluding to?"

"You won't have to deal with customers, who, as I'm sure you can remember, often bought your work only because it was the right size for a particular hallway or was done in colors that matched those in a living room, after haggling with you on price. And you won't have to put up with superficial spectators, who look at your work and make broad, sweeping, all inclusive comments such as, 'That's nice' or 'That's colorful.' Nor will you have to put up with the artsy-fartsy phonies who want only to demonstrate their own artistic prowess while supposedly appreciating your work."

"Is there a hell?"

"Not in the sense that you probably mean, with devils, fire, and pitchforks. It's simply a boring, unartistic life, the kind led by billions of people who pass through an earthly existence with no appreciation of the beauty around them and no desire to create something equal to it. Just as you and other artists made a kind of heaven every time you created art, so too did your antitheses create their own hell—every time they did not look up to see a leaf shaking in the wind; stood before a painting in a gallery or museum and failed to think about a particular brush stroke, instead thinking only about what's for lunch; or heard beautiful music on the car radio but switched to the local station doing sports coverage. You and the other artists get to stay here. The others have to return and live mushed together in a world where they'll never do anything creative. They'd rather argue over doctrine, canonical law, who's right, who's wrong, and carry out lots of repetitive rites and ceremonies, including handling snakes and walking on hot coals. They'll try lots of proselyting to win the others to their own side, and if that doesn't work, they'll go to war with each other."

"I have to ask. How did you get in? I know you wrote a couple of books for the Christian Bible, The Book of Luke and the Acts of the Apostles. Did that do it?"

"I actually was a painter, too. I did some portraits of Mary, Jesus, Peter, Paul, most of the biggies in the New Testament. Plus I showed up in some paintings done by other artists, like *Luke and the Madonna*. I guess that counts for something. At any rate, I got assigned to be the greeter/guardian/gate keeper here."

"I know this is a sensitive subject for lots of Christians, but did Jesus make it in? I never read in the Bible that he did watercolors or made quilts."

"He is of course here. He was one of those we praised earlier for composing pieces with layers of meaning, particularly in his parables. 'The Sermon on the Mount' was a real gem. How can anyone forget 'Blessed are the peacemakers'? And remember, he was a carpenter, who created lots of works in wood. Plus, I'd give him the benefit of the doubt for all his suffering and death at the hands of a group who claimed he had broken their rules while trying to do good for his people."

"So, I'm in? I made it?"

"Yes. Now go explore and then create. Use your imagination. You've got all the supplies necessary to get started, and, more importantly, you've got all the time you need."

About the Author

Joseph Meigs was born in Atlanta, Georgia, and raised in Berkeley, California, and Jacksonville, Florida. He earned a B.A (1964) in English with minors in chemistry and biology while attending the University of Florida on a basketball scholarship. He received his PhD in English there in 1970 and went on to teach literature (Shakespeare, World Literature, and Literary Criticism) and film studies at Western Carolina University until retiring in 2005. He has been a photographer and watercolor painter for approximately thirty-five years, currently serving as one of the resident artists for the Jackson County (North Carolina) Arts Association. His favorite subjects are old barns, cabins, and landscapes. He is the author of the novel *Tenure Track* (a satire about the hurdles one must jump to receive a favorable decision on tenure, published in 2002) and *Death Without Dignity* (a comic murder mystery, published in 2010). He has enjoyed tennis, skiing, golf, running, and restoring Datsun 240Z's. He is married with three sons.